the holiday frenzy, allow me to prescribe this delightful antidote to be taken cuddled up by a roaring fire while sipping a steaming cup of peppermint tea."

—Bookreporter

"Rings in Christmas in tried-and-true Macomber style, with romance and a touch of heavenly magic."
—*Kirkus Reviews*

"[A] sweetly charming holiday romance."
—*Library Journal*

"I absolutely loved this latest tale from Ms. Macomber. She has such a way of telling an entertaining story and sprinkling just enough angst and/or humor throughout the pages to make her readers never want to put one of her books down. . . . Packed with madcap antics, this is a holiday story you'll treasure over and over again throughout the years. I highly recommend it!"
—Night Owl Romance (Top Pick)

"In this joyous and whimsical holiday novel, Debbie Macomber rings in the season with the return of Shirley, Goodness, and Mercy, delivering laughs, love, and a charming dose of angelic intervention. . . . An unforgettable Christmas miracle."
—Fresh Fiction

"A witty, touching contemporary romance that will have you sighing and leave you with a smile on your face. . . . Macomber has penned a delightful story that is sure to steal your heart."
—Romance Junkies

The Inn at Rose Harbor

"Debbie Macomber's Cedar Cove romance novels have a warm, comfy feel to them. Perhaps that's why they've sold millions."
—*USA Today*

"No one tugs at readers' heartstrings quite as effectively as Macomber."
—*Chicago Tribune*

"The characters and their various entanglements are sure to resonate with Macomber fans. . . . The book sets up an appealing milieu of townspeople and visitors that sets the stage for what will doubtless be many further adventures at the Inn at Rose Harbor."
—*The Seattle Times*

"Debbie Macomber is the reigning queen of women's fiction."
—*The Sacramento Bee*

"A warm and cosy read that tugs at the heartstrings, with love and redemption blooming when it is least expected."
—*The Toowoomba Chronicle* (Australia)

"The prolific Macomber introduces a spin-off of sorts from her popular Cedar Cove series, still set in that fictional small town but centered on Jo Marie Rose, a youngish widow who buys and operates the bed and breakfast of the title. This clever premise allows Macomber to craft stories around the B&B's guests, Abby and Josh in this inaugural effort, while using Jo Marie and her ongoing recovery from the death of her husband Paul in Afghanistan as the series' anchor. . . . With her characteristic optimism, Macomber provides fresh starts for both."
—*Booklist*

"Emotionally charged romance."
—*Kirkus Reviews*

For a complete list of books by Debbie Macomber,
visit her website at
www.debbiemacomber.com.

DEBBIE MACOMBER

Angels at the Table

A Shirley, Goodness, and Mercy
Christmas Story

BALLANTINE BOOKS

NEW YORK

2013 Ballantine Books Mass Market Edition

Copyright © 2012 by Debbie Macomber
Excerpt from *Starry Night* by Debbie Macomber copyright © 2013 by Debbie Macomber

Published in the United States by Ballantine Books, an imprint of The Random House Publishing Group, a division of Random House LLC, a Penguin Random House Company, New York.

BALLANTINE and the HOUSE colophon are registered trademarks of Random House LLC.

Originally published in hardcover in the United States by Ballantine Books, an imprint of The Random House Publishing Group, a division of Random House LLC, in 2012.

This book contains an excerpt from the forthcoming book *Starry Night* by Debbie Macomber. This excerpt has been set for this edition only and may not reflect the final content of the forthcoming edition.

ISBN 978-0-345-52888-9
eISBN 978-0-345-53596-2

Cover design: Lynn Andreozzi
Cover illustration: Tom Hallman

Printed in the United States of America

www.ballantinebooks.com

9 8 7 6 5 4 3 2 1

Ballantine mass market edition: November 2013

To
Diane DeGooyer Harmon
and
Kathy Huard

Two special angels God
sent into my life when
I needed them most

November 2012

Dear friends,

They're back! For the last three years I've read every form of communication available asking me when I was going to write another Shirley, Goodness, and Mercy book. Well, my friends, here it is, three years in the making. This time my trio is visiting New York, and as usual they're up to their antics, causing all kinds of havoc and involving themselves in human affairs. Really, they just can't stop themselves.

This book is special because I am introducing another angel. His name is Will and he is the result of a letter I received from a reader several years ago. Rose Williamson suggested I should have an angel named Will. I remember frowning when I read her letter and thinking to myself, "Why would I want to add an angel and why would I name him Will?" As I continued reading, Rose said, "Seeing that you based the angels on the Bible verse from the 23rd Psalm that says, 'Surely, goodness and mercy *will* follow you . . .'" Immediately, Will, an apprentice angel, was born in my mind, thanks to this clever reader who shared a great idea with me. Thank you, Rose!

Escape the craziness of the season, settle back with a cup of hot tea and a Christmas goodie, and put your feet up.

Relax and be prepared to laugh and, if you happen to see a camel wandering down the street all on its own, you can take a guess on just who might be behind that mischief.

Have a wonderful Christmas.

Debbie Macomber

P.S. I always love hearing from my readers, so please don't hesitate to contact me. You can reach me through my website at DebbieMacomber.com or Facebook at DebbieMacomberWorld or through the mail at P.O. Box 1458, Port Orchard, WA 98366. I value your comments and suggestions.

Angels at the Table

Chapter One

"This is really Earth?" Will, the apprentice angel, asked, lying on his stomach on a low-flying cloud with his three mentors. His eyes widened as he gazed down on the crazed activity below.

"This is Earth," Mercy informed their young charge with a tinge of pride. For all its problems, Earth was a fascinating place to visit, with the tall buildings that butted up against the sky and people milling about with such purpose, most of them unaware of the spiritual world that surrounded them. More times than she could remember Mercy had lost patience with humans. Those who were considered the apex of God's creations appeared to be slow-witted and spiritually dull. Yet she loved them and treasured her Earthly assignments.

"It's New York," Shirley added, resting her chin in her hands as she gazed longingly below. "Oh, I do so love this city."

"Manhattan, to be more precise," Goodness clarified and ended with a little sigh, indicating that she, too, had missed visiting Earth.

The four hovered near Times Square, watching the clamoring crowds jockeying for space on New Year's Eve.

Will's eyes widened as he intently studied the scene taking place in the streets below. "Is it always like this—so busy and crowded, I mean?"

"No, no, this is a special night. The people are gathering together to usher in the New Year." Time was a concept reserved for Earth. In heaven it was much different. Consequently, the time restriction placed on the three Prayer Ambassadors when given Earthly assignments had caused more than one problem.

"Did Gabriel want us—"

"Gabriel," Shirley gasped, and quickly cut him off. "He doesn't exactly know that we've brought you here. It would probably be best if you didn't mention this short visit to him, okay?"

"Yes, please, it would be best not to let *anyone* know we've shown you Earth." It went without saying they'd be in all kinds of trouble if Gabriel learned what they'd been up to.

"Gabriel means well but he tends to get a little prickly about these things," Goodness explained to their young charge.

"Why is that?" Will stared at all three of them.

"Well, you see, we . . . the three of us . . . thought we should give you a bird's-eye view of Earth and these people God loves so much—strictly for training purposes." Mercy looked to her friends to expound upon their intentions, which were honorable if not a tad bit sneaky.

This Earthly visitation had been a spur-of-the-moment decision. Mercy had been the one to suggest it. Naturally, Goodness was quick to agree, and after some discussion Shirley had seen the light as well.

Will, an apprentice angel, had been placed under their charge, and given this honor, it was only right that he get a glimpse of the trials and tribulations that awaited him once he started working as a Prayer Ambassador. The job could be a bit tricky, and the more Will understood the idiosyncrasies of humans, the better he would do once given an assignment from Gabriel.

Mercy was certain that under their tutorship, Will would make a fine Prayer Ambassador one day. He was young and enthusiastic, eager to learn about Earth and the role he would play.

As Mercy, who had falsely been labeled a troublemaker, had pointed out, theirs was a duty that required serious dedication. She wasn't alone in believing this. Goodness—oh, poor Goodness—had gotten something of a reputation, too, and Mercy felt partially to blame, but that was another story entirely. Shirley tended to be a bit more on the straight-and-narrow path and had worked hard to reform her friends. In fact, Shirley, a former Guardian Angel, had done such a marvelous job, Gabriel had offered to let them train the promising young angel who was with them now.

Naturally, it was understood that if the three of them accepted this assignment training Will, then of course there would be no hanky-panky, no tricks, no nothing. All three had agreed. This was a high honor indeed and their intentions were good.

Now here they were, New Year's Eve in Times Square, in one of the most amazing cities on Earth. Mercy breathed in deeply, savoring the moment. Bringing Will had been a good excuse, but the fact of the matter was that she had missed visiting Earth. It'd been a good long while since their last assignment, and she missed the razzle-dazzle of the big city.

"Isn't Earth just marvelous?" Goodness said, her huge wings fluttering with delight. "Just look at all those neon lights. I've always been especially fond of light."

"As we all are," Shirley reminded them.

"Can we go down there with the people?" Will asked.

"Absolutely not." Shirley's loud protest was instantaneous.

"I don't think it would hurt anything," Goodness countered, her gaze still fixed on the bright lights of the city below.

Will glanced from one to the other.

"How will he ever learn about humans if he doesn't have the opportunity to mingle with them?" Mercy asked, siding with her dearest friend. Shirley could be such a stickler for rules. Okay, so they'd originally promised not to get anywhere close to humans, but this would be a good teaching moment for Will.

"How will he ever learn how to work as a Prayer Ambassador if he doesn't become familiar with humans?" Goodness protested.

Shirley wavered. While she might be opinionated on a number of topics, she could be easily swayed, which was the best part of working with her, Mercy felt.

"Well . . ."

"Do we hear the humans' prayers?" Will asked.

"Oh, no," Shirley explained. "Only God hears their prayers, and then He talks matters over with Gabriel and then . . ."

"Then Gabriel passes along those requests to us."

"And we assist in answering them."

"One of our roles is to help humans realize how much they can do for themselves with God's help," Goodness clarified.

"We try as best we can without *interfering* in their lives," Shirley added quickly, glaring at Goodness and Mercy.

This was a warning and Mercy recognized it the instant her friend spoke.

"But first, and this is the most important part," Goodness emphasized, "it's our duty to teach these humans a lesson. Then and only then are we able to help them with their troubles.

"The real difficulty comes when they don't want to learn." Goodness shook her head because this aspect of the job was often a challenge. "Some people seem to want God to step in and do as they ask without making a single contribution to the effort."

"It doesn't work like that," Mercy said, although she'd done a fair bit of finagling to help these poor witless souls. In theory, answering prayers didn't sound the least bit difficult. Unfortunately, humans were sometimes completely dense.

"They can be so stubborn," Goodness said, shaking her head again.

"Strong willed," Shirley agreed.

"Oh, yes, and once—" Mercy snapped her mouth closed. It was best not to reveal their past antics for fear it would mislead their young charge into thinking that perhaps he should follow in their footsteps. Gabriel would take exception to that.

"Once?" Will pressed. "What happened?"

"Never mind," Shirley said, reading the situation perfectly. "Some things are best laid to rest and not discussed."

"Can I go down and be with the crowd?" Will asked again. "I won't say anything to Gabriel."

"He isn't the only one," Shirley blurted out. "I mean, we shouldn't mutter a word of this to anyone in heaven."

"Or Earth," Goodness reminded them all.

"We can't speak to humans?" Will frowned as though confused.

"We can but only . . ."

"But definitely not tonight," Shirley said so fast her voice rose an entire octave.

Mercy took Will's hand. "There have been times over the last two millenniums when we have spoken directly to humans."

"Those occasions have been rare, however."

"Yes, very rare."

"But not as rare as they should have been," Shirley found it necessary to add. She crossed her arms over her chest and seemed to be wavering about the best way to handle this training session.

"I don't think it would hurt for Will to go down in the crowd," Goodness said again. "It is a very special night here on Earth."

"I promise not to say a word to anyone, human or otherwise," Will assured them.

It was hard to refuse him when Mercy was itching to mingle herself. It'd been quite a while since she'd visited Earth, and humans had long fascinated her.

"Let's do it." Goodness rubbed her palms together, as eager as Mercy.

"I . . . don't know."

Mercy ignored the former Guardian Angel. "I'm off. Will," she shouted, "follow me and stay close. Do what I do." She zoomed down toward Times

Square with Will on one side and Goodness on the other.

"No, no . . . this could be a mistake," Shirley shouted before speeding off to catch up with them. "Do as I do," she added.

The four landed behind a concrete barrier with several people pressed up against it. Policemen stood on the opposite side, patrolling the crowd, looking for any signs of a disruption.

"Can they hear us?" Will whispered.

"Only those with spiritual ears who are attuned to God," Shirley answered. "And even then they will doubt themselves."

"No one is listening now." Mercy was fairly confident the crowd was too caught up in the excitement of the moment to notice their presence, which was for the best all around.

"How come they're bundled up with coats and scarves and gloves?" Will asked, looking around.

"It's winter."

"Oh."

"Everyone is staring up at the giant clock," Will observed.

"Yes, it's only a couple of minutes until the new year arrives."

"And that's important?"

"Oh, yes. In two minutes this year will be over and a new one will begin." This would be a hard concept for Will to understand. All their young charge knew came from heaven, where there were no clocks or calendars. In heaven, time had no meaning; the past, present, and the future were all one and the same.

The restrictions of time had always been problematic to Mercy. Gabriel generally gave them a limited amount of time to help humans with their prayer requests, and staying within such a condensed time period often seemed impossible. Although, through their many experiences, Mercy had learned that with God all things were possible. That had been a powerful lesson and one she hoped to pass along to Will when the opportunity arose.

"How come the streets are black?" Will asked, gazing down at his feet.

"They aren't gold here."

"It's asphalt. Earth is nothing like heaven," Mercy explained. If Will stuck around Earth much longer, other differences would soon become apparent.

"Where's Shirley?" Goodness whirled around so quickly she caused a small whirlwind to form. People grabbed on to their hats. Papers flew in every direction. "We've lost Shirley."

"No, we haven't." For Will's sake Mercy made every attempt to remain calm. "I'm sure she's close by."

"She isn't."

"Oh dear," Will cried. "Shirley's disappeared."

"She's got to be right here." Mercy was beginning to grow frantic herself. This wasn't good. Shirley was older and tended to be easily sidetracked, but vanishing like this wasn't the least bit like her. Of the three of them, Shirley was by far the most responsible.

"Look for children," Mercy instructed Goodness and Will. Shirley was invariably drawn to little ones. It was a result of all the years she'd spent as a Guardian Angel.

Mercy scanned the crowd then rose above the street and peered down, hoping for a glimpse of her friend.

Goodness joined her. "Do you see her?"

"Do you?"

"No."

Mercy continued looking and when she turned to connect with Goodness, her friend was gone as well. Panic was starting to take hold. "Will," she shouted, fearing she'd lost complete control of the situation.

"I'm here."

Thank heaven for that. "Do you see Goodness?"

"What about Shirley?"

Shirley wasn't nearly the worry Goodness was. If her fellow Prayer Ambassador got loose there was no telling the trouble she could get into. And Goodness could do it without even trying.

"Is that Goodness over by those people on the stand?" Will asked.

Stand? What stand? Mercy surveyed the area until she saw the direction Will indicated. This was exactly what she'd feared. Goodness had gotten distracted by the television crew busily working the cameras. It was all those lights. Goodness found lights impossible to resist.

Mercy arrived in the nick of time. Goodness also had a weakness for anything electronic. Everything in heaven was advanced and her fellow angel was fascinated by the primitive forms of communication still commonly used on Earth.

"Goodness," Mercy screeched. "Don't do it."

Startled, Goodness disappeared from the jumbo screen but not before her shadowy image briefly flashed across the surface. A hush fell over the crowd.

"Did you see that?" someone shouted and pointed at the screen.

"It looked like an angel."

"It's a sign from God."

Mercy groaned. This was worse than she'd imagined. If word of this got back to Gabriel they could all be banned from Earth forever.

"I knew something like this was bound to happen." Shirley appeared out of the blue, hands digging into her hips. Her face was crunched up into a look of righteous indignation.

"We were looking for you," Mercy admonished before Shirley could complain. "Where did you go?"

"I was around."

"Goodness." Shirley grabbed hold of the Prayer Ambassador just before she made a repeat appearance on the big screen.

"She can't help herself." Mercy felt obliged to defend her dearest friend.

"Where's Will?"

Sure enough Will was now nowhere to be seen.

"I'll find him." But first Mercy had to take care of Goodness.

"I know, I know," Shirley said, catching hold of Goodness a second time. "I'll get her back to heaven. You find Will."

"Where were you?" Mercy demanded, unwilling to let Shirley off without an explanation.

"Sorry, I saw a cranky toddler. Mom was doing her best to soothe her with little success, so I lent her a hand. The little boy is fast asleep now."

"Thanks to you."

"I've learned a fair number of lullabies in my time."

No doubt Shirley had.

"I'll join you as soon as I can." Mercy caught a glimpse of Will out of the corner of her eye. As she suspected, he'd returned to the street. The crowd started to chant off the seconds and then a loud, joyous cry arose as the mass of people welcomed in the New Year.

"Happy New Year," Shirley cried out as she escorted Goodness home.

"Happy New Year," Mercy echoed. Now all she had to do was collect Will before he got into trouble.

Oh dear . . . oh dear. It looked like she was too late.

Humans surrounded her, hugging and kissing, and there was Will, standing beside two people all alone with their backs to each other.

Mercy could see what was about to happen and felt powerless to stop it. With a single nudge of his wing, Will caused these two strangers to stumble into each other.

Chapter Two

Lucie Ferrara knew it would be a mistake to come to Times Square on New Year's Eve. She'd so much rather be curled up in bed with a good book.

What had she been thinking?

Instead of indulging herself with a good read, Lucie had let Jazmine and Catherine talk her into going with them into the madhouse of this New Year's Eve celebration. Lucie's own mother had teamed up against her, insisting Lucie worked too hard. She needed to get out of the house and enjoy herself with her friends.

Some fun this had turned out to be. Jazmine and Catherine were nowhere to be found and Lucie was trapped in this huge mass of humanity, unable to move in any direction. People pressed against her from all sides and all she wanted to do was escape. The subway station was within sight and if she could simply make her way . . .

All at once the crowd started to shout. A cacophony of noise erupted all around her as a cheer rose and "Auld Lang Syne" was blasted through the cold night air.

To make her feel even more alone, all the couples around her were either hugging or kissing. Everyone seemed to belong to someone. Everyone, that is, except her.

Unable to watch and feeling detached, Lucie closed her eyes. Her mother had wanted her to enjoy herself with her friends. It'd been weeks since Lucie had been out. She needed a free night, Wendy had gently reminded her. All work and no play would cause her to lose her focus.

Her mother, however, was right. Lucie did need a break, and she probably did work too hard. Putting a restaurant together wasn't a simple thing. There were decisions to be made and compromises, too. They'd found a great location in Brooklyn, not far from their apartment. While the space was perfect for what they needed, renovations were necessary and permits took time, money, and effort.

Furthermore, Lucie had a responsibility to her mother, who had invested the entire life insurance money they'd collected from her father's death into making this restaurant a success. Her mother's faith in her was both a blessing and a curse. If Lucie failed she'd never be able to forgive herself.

Suddenly Lucie was jarred from behind. She stumbled forward. "Oh, sorry."

"Sorry."

Her eyes flashed open, the apology already spoken, when she stared into the face of the most amazingly good-looking man she'd seen outside of a movie. He was taller than she by a good six inches and had the warmest, gentlest brown eyes. A lock of dark brown hair fell across his wide forehead.

"You okay?" he asked. "The crowd . . ."

"I know; it's crazy. No worries, I'm fine."

His hands braced her shoulders as if to catch her from stumbling. He didn't drop them, and for the longest time they simply stared at each other. Surprisingly, he didn't seem to be coupled with anyone. He was alone in the crowd, too.

"Shall we?" he asked.

Not fully understanding, she blinked.

Then with barely a pause, he lowered his mouth to hers.

Standing on the tips of her toes, Lucie wrapped her arms around his neck and welcomed his kiss. Why not? It was New Year's Eve and this was tradition.

The kiss lasted through what remained of the song, and Lucie enjoyed it immensely. The earth didn't move, the sky didn't fall, but the exchange was warm, soft, and above all pleasant. Very pleasant. She almost groaned in protest when they broke apart.

He smiled at her.

Lucie smiled back.

"I'm Aren Fairchild."

"Lucie Ferrara."

The crowd started to break apart. The people that had been standing so close just seconds before were leaving. All at once it seemed everyone had somewhere else to go.

Lucie and Aren remained motionless, standing in the same spot. He continued to cup her shoulders.

"I got separated from my sister," he explained. "I don't have a clue what happened to Jazmine and Catherine."

"So you're alone?"

Lucie nodded.

"I am, too. Perhaps we can find a place for a glass of wine?"

"I'd like that." Her heart fluttered with gentle excitement at his invitation. Maybe, just maybe, this entire evening wouldn't be a disaster after all.

Lucie's phone chirped, indicating she had a text message. Digging in her purse she retrieved it and saw that the text was from Jazmine. Where are you?

Lucie quickly texted her back. Still in Times Square.

C and I R heading to the subway.

Talk tomorrow.

OK

When Lucie finished she noticed Aren was busy tapping away on his phone, too. He glanced up when he'd set his phone inside his coat pocket. "I let my sister know I'd find my own way home."

"I told my friends the same thing."

He reached for her hand and off they went. After a number of attempts to find available space at a wine bar, they gave up and settled for a booth in an all-night diner.

It felt good to sit down. Lucie shrugged off her coat. Aren unbuttoned his overcoat.

"I'm sorry. I'm unfamiliar with the area or I'd know of a place."

"I doubt it would have mattered," Lucie assured him. "On a night like this every seat is taken. We were lucky to get a table here." After she spoke she realized he must be new to the city. "You're not from New York?"

"Seattle," he explained.

In other words he was a tourist. Well, that was probably for the best, seeing that she didn't really have time to invest in a relationship, if indeed this turned into one. Oh dear, she was getting way ahead of herself.

"I recently moved to the city."

"Oh." Instantly her spirits lifted, even though her circumstances weren't going to change for a long while.

"What about you?"

"I live in Brooklyn."

"I haven't been there yet, but my sister tells me it's fast becoming the place to be. I'll need to find an apartment soon and she suggested I look there."

"You'll like it." Lucie had lived in Brooklyn her entire life and was part of the community. Their apartment was just off Jamison Street. Their restaurant, once they opened, would be relatively close. They'd decided to name it Heavenly Delights.

"What brings you to New York?" she asked.

"A job. I'm a writer and a good friend recommended me for a position with the *New York Gazette*."

"The *Gazette*. Wow, you must be very good."

"I'd like to think so, but time will tell. What about you?"

Lucie hardly knew where to start. "Well, I recently graduated from culinary school, and my mother and I are working toward opening a restaurant."

It looked as if Aren was about to say something but changed his mind. "That takes a lot of work."

"Tell me about it." She stopped herself from elaborating on the trials and difficulties, the expense and the fears. This wasn't the time for that.

"You're looking thoughtful," Aren commented.

Lucie smiled. "Just before we bumped into each other I was thinking that I'd much rather be home than standing alone in the cold."

Aren chuckled. "Funny, I was thinking the same thing. The only reason I agreed to go was because I didn't want my sister to be alone. She had a recent breakup and is taking it pretty hard. Actually, I was wondering if I'd find my way back to my sister's apartment."

"You're lost?"

"Not exactly," he said and looked a bit embarrassed. "Understanding these street directions is driving me nuts and testing my intelligence. What do you mean when you say on Fifty-third between Sixth and Seventh when the address is something completely different, like twelve Madison Avenue? I used to think I had a good sense of direction. No longer."

Now it was Lucie's turn to laugh. "Don't worry, you'll catch on soon enough."

"I hope so."

The harried waitress approached their table and handed them menus. "Coffee?"

"Please," Lucie answered. She was going to need it if she intended to stay awake much longer, and she sincerely hoped that she was. Her day had started at four that morning, meeting with contractors and dealing with what seemed like a dozen problems that all had to be resolved that day.

Aren righted his coffee mug and glanced at the menu. "I don't generally eat this late, but Josie insisted we'd find something on the street."

Josie must be his sister. "And you ended up not eating."

"The truth is I spent half the evening in a frantic search for my sister. We were continually separated."

That had happened to Lucie as well with her two friends. The cops had directed them into a fenced-off area, but the crowd still seemed to move her away from her friends. She probably should have been a bit more aggressive, but that simply wasn't her nature. And she was nervous to leave her spot because she knew the cops wouldn't let her back in.

"What do you hope for the new year?" Aren asked, after sipping his coffee.

"Oh my, so much." Lucie sat up straighter and talked nonstop for a good ten minutes, until she realized she'd completely dominated the conversation. More than a little embarrassed, she shook her head. "Enough about me. What do you hope for the new year?"

"No, no, continue," he insisted, and then added, "Actually, there's something important I'm waiting to hear."

"And what would that be?"

His smile was warm. "What about the men in your life?"

Lucie shrugged. "At the moment there's only one."

"So, there's someone important in your life?"

"He's a bit possessive, too."

Aren's smile faded. "Really? Tell me about him."

"His name is Sammy, and we've been together five years. Actually, he lets me sleep with him."

"I beg your pardon?" Aren laid the menu aside and frowned.

"Sammy's a fifteen-pound mixed-breed dog my mother and I adopted. He does allow me to sleep with him and makes sure I know I am there only by his generosity."

Aren laughed. "In other words you're currently not involved with anyone . . . human."

"Correct." Lucie was thrilled he'd asked. "What about you? Any women in your life?"

He sighed heavily. "I'm two years out of a divorce." He looked down at his coffee.

Lucie watched as the sadness and disappointment sank Aren's shoulders.

"Katie and I were married for five years. She fell in love with someone else." He said it as if the pain lingered still.

"Children?"

"No, thankfully we avoided that complication. I wanted a family but Katie kept coming up with excuses. In retrospect, I'm grateful."

"Have you dated much since?"

"Very little. But getting back to you, because I want this to be clear between us. You're not involved with a man, or currently married, right?" He posed the question as if he feared a repeat of the mistakes in his past. "You see, the man Katie left me for was someone she was once involved with."

"Oh, no worries there."

He frowned now. "Why not? You're wonderful."

She blushed with his praise. "No time. First, it was because I was in culinary school and working part-time to pay tuition. And now, well, now Mom and I are struggling to get our restaurant up and running. There simply aren't enough hours in the day to do all that needs to be done, let alone have much of a social life."

The waitress returned to the table for their orders

and they each chose a light breakfast. The conversation didn't lag once.

Their plates had long since been removed and they'd each drank two or three additional cups of coffee before Lucie happened to glance at her watch and notice the time.

"My goodness, it's almost four," she gasped as her hand flew to her heart. The hours had simply evaporated. She found it shocking to realize they'd been sitting in the all-night diner for the better part of three and a half hours.

With a sense of panic Lucie reached for her purse, and slid out of the booth. "I have to work today." She couldn't believe she'd let the time get away from her like this. She'd be fortunate to get three hours' sleep before working a twelve-hour shift. Her mother had urged her to take New Year's Day off, but Lucie didn't feel she could refuse the extra hours. Not when the restaurant paid time and a half for working the holiday. They could use the money.

Right now every penny counted. Their goal was to open Heavenly Delights on March first, but seeing how much time everything took, Lucie had come to realize that that was an optimistic estimate.

Aren reached for her hand. "Let me walk you to the subway."

"Okay." She didn't want to leave, but she really didn't have a choice. As it was, Lucie had already been up for the last twenty-four hours. "I don't mean to rush away but . . ."

"It's all right, I understand."

"Oh, Aren, I can't remember when I've enjoyed myself more. You're so easy to talk to." For a good portion of their evening she'd found herself sharing with him things she hadn't told her coworkers and friends. Her eyes had filled with tears as she spoke of her father, who had passed away eighteen months earlier of complications from what should have been a routine surgery.

Her brother lived and worked in Texas and had a young family, so it was just Lucie and her mother. And Wendy had health issues of her own. As a type 1 diabetic, Lucie's mother had to carefully watch her diet and insulin levels.

Aren reached for his overcoat. "I was just thinking how interesting and fun you are."

He'd already taken care of their tab, so they were free to leave.

"I'd like to see you again," he said as they walked down the sidewalk toward the subway station.

"I'd like that, too, but . . ."

"But," he said, finishing the thought for her, "you don't know if a relationship is possible just now."

"Yes." She was grateful he'd put it into words for her.

"I understand, but we both just said what a good time we've had. I don't think we should be so willing to simply walk away from each other. The least we could do is get to know each other a little better. I can't speak for you, but this is the first time in two years that I've felt like myself. I'm starting over and I've met someone wonderful and I don't want it to end after one night." His steps slowed to match hers as they continued walking. "According to my sister I'm a great guy and—"

"You are a great guy."

"And I happen to think you're pretty wonderful yourself, so what do you say?"

They arrived outside the subway station and Lucie hesitated.

"Can I kiss you again?" he asked. "Maybe that will persuade you."

"Yes, please." She leaned toward him and automatically slipped her arms around his neck.

Their first exchange had been pleasant. The second, after coming to know each other a bit more, was several multiples better. This time she did hear music, but it was the sound of a happy heart.

As soon as they broke apart she realized how badly she didn't want to abandon this fledgling relationship.

Aren held her gaze, awaiting her response. Bracing his forehead against hers he offered a suggestion. "Tell you what."

"What?"

"Rather than walk away, give this some thought, okay?"

"What do you mean?"

"I think I know what you're thinking. We're high

on emotion and caffeine, and more than a little exhausted."

That had been exactly her thought process.

"Take a week."

"A week," she repeated.

"If you decide this feeling is something you're interested in exploring then we'll meet again on January seventh at four o'clock."

"January seventh at four o'clock," she repeated.

"Seven days," he repeated, "to think this through properly."

At the moment seven days seemed entirely too long to wait. Lucie was ready to make her decision right then and there, feeling as she did now. Still, a heavy responsibility had fallen onto her shoulders in regard to this restaurant. Now wasn't the time to get involved with someone, even if that someone was as wonderful as Aren.

"Where should we meet?" Lucie asked. "At the diner again?"

"No," he said, and ran his finger down the side of her face. "I'll admit I'm a bit of a romantic. Let's meet at the top of the Empire State Building."

"Why there?" she asked, smiling at his suggestion.

"That's where I'd like to kiss you again."

"Okay," she agreed, "but you understand . . . I might not come. I hate the thought of you just waiting for me there in the cold."

"Then don't keep me waiting."

"Oh, Aren, I don't know . . ."

"Not now you don't. Give it a week? Okay?"

"Okay."

Aren walked her down the stairs to the subway and waited with her until her train arrived. Lucie stepped inside and automatically went to the window, pressing her hand against it. Standing on the other side, Aren pressed his palm against hers, with the glass between them. As the train started to move, she blew him a kiss.

How wise he was. A week would give her time to think, time to decide. And how romantic of him to suggest the top of the Empire State Building. Biting down on her lower lip, Lucie wanted so badly to continue their relationship . . . but the timing was all wrong. Yet, would she ever have a chance like this again? That was a question she was afraid to answer.

Chapter Three

Lucie's eyes burned as she hurriedly dressed for work after less than three hours' sleep. Even though she was physically dragging, emotionally she was on an all-time high. She didn't harbor a single regret. Her trip into the city had been amazing. Meeting Aren had set her heart spinning with possibilities. They'd clicked as if they'd grown up together, rediscovering a deep connection to each other after a long separation.

Before her father died, and before Lucie had started culinary school, she'd dated often. With other men there'd always been that awkward getting-to-know-you period with long pauses in conversation as they struggled to find a connection. It hadn't been that way with Aren. He'd been so interesting and interested in her. She'd never met a man who wasn't keen on talking about himself, dominating the conversation and looking to make an impression. Aren had been so comfortable with who he was that he didn't seem to feel the need to babble on and on about his career or his influential friends. The connection had been there from the very first, which made her decision all the more difficult. How could she walk away from this promising relationship? How would it be possible to maintain even the semblance of one, stretched for time as she already was?

Lucie ran a brush through her dark, shoulder-length hair and then pinned it away from her face, looping the long strands behind her ears. Once she was in the restaurant kitchen, she'd secure it with a net and a chef's hat. She wore the hat with pride. She'd worked hard for the privilege.

Her mother paused in the doorway to Lucie's bathroom. "What time did you get in last night?"

"Late." Lucie wasn't about to tell her mother exactly what time she'd slipped into bed.

"Did you have fun?"

Sighing, Lucie nodded. "I had the most amazing night."

Her mother's face brightened. "I knew getting out would do you a world of good. Lucie, I worry about you and all the hours you work. I'm happy you took my advice and went out with your friends."

"I'm happy I did, too. Don't worry about me, really, Mom, it won't be like this much longer." Once the restaurant was up and running Lucie would be able to take a breather. She hoped. Heavenly Delights needed to be a success. It was their future, their dream, and Lucie was determined to make it a winner. She simply had to, seeing that her mother had invested so heavily in it. Wendy had trusted

Lucie with her life's savings and life insurance money and Lucie couldn't, wouldn't, disappoint her family.

"You met someone, didn't you?"

"Mom!"

"Didn't you?"

Reluctantly, Lucie nodded.

"Why so secretive? Tell me about him."

"Mom, I don't have time. I'm late already."

Her mother remained undeterred. "Well, at least tell me how you met."

Lucie couldn't have contained a smile if she'd tried. "We met in Times Square at midnight and Aren kissed me."

Wendy's eyes widened. "Well, of course. That's how I met all the men in my life," she teased.

"I lost Jazmine and Catherine in the crowd and I was standing alone while everyone was ringing in the New Year. People were singing, hugging, and kissing one another. Aren and I bumped against each other and before I knew it we were kissing, too."

Her mother's shoulders rose with a deep sigh. "That is probably the most romantic thing I've ever heard."

Lucie finished putting on her makeup, took one last look at herself in the mirror, and decided it was good enough. Once she was finished with work, she'd eat a light dinner and go straight to bed. She needed to be careful in the kitchen, working around knives and fire while sleep deprived.

"When are you seeing Aren again?" her mother asked, following Lucie into the kitchen.

"I . . . I don't know. He's new in town and busy."

"Lucie . . ."

"Yes, Mom?" she said, forcing a light tone into her voice.

Her mother faced her, hands on her hips. "You're not telling me something. I told you when you were just a girl that you don't need to be afraid to tell me anything. I'm your mother."

"And you're the best mother in the world, too," she said and kissed Wendy's cheek.

"But . . ." her mother protested.

"I'll tell you more after work, okay?" Lucie didn't have time to chat, and besides, she wasn't sure how little or how much to explain. That warm feeling had stayed with her through the night. Her dreams had been full of Aren. He'd been so certain, confident they should meet again. Although he had given her only a few details of his divorce, she knew he'd been badly hurt. Yet he was willing to set aside his fears for her, and in essence was asking her to overlook the obstacles in her life and give them a chance.

Aren was new to the city, looking to make a new life for himself. And he wanted to start by dating her. Her mind continued to buzz with questions, with doubts, with longing and fears. The newspaper probably had a probation period for its writers. Their meeting and the instant attraction they'd experienced had come as a surprise. To Aren as much as Lucie. Neither had expected anything like this. Still, the timing couldn't be worse.

"You're looking thoughtful, sweetheart," her mother said, cutting into Lucie's thoughts. "Are you sure there isn't something you want to tell me now?"

"I'm sure." Lucie forced herself to smile. "Just that Aren is simply wonderful."

Her mother gripped Lucie's hand. "It's time you found someone, Lucie. At your age I was already married and pregnant with your brother."

"Stop, Mom, you make me sound like Aunt Adele."

"She didn't marry until she was forty-three," Wendy reminded her.

"Yes, but Aunt Adele traveled the globe, swam with stingrays, started two companies, and married when she found the man she couldn't live without. I haven't met that man yet."

"How do you know?" her mother challenged. "It could be Aren. Give him a chance, Lucie. It's been a long time since I've seen your eyes sparkle like this when you talked about a man. I haven't even met this Aren and already I like him."

Rather than comment, Lucie grabbed her purse and headed out the door. Her mother could be right, but she didn't have time to think about any of this just now.

Once she was at work Lucie was so busy the hours passed by with incredible speed. At the end of her shift, she was exhausted to the point she could barely think straight. On the subway ride home, she nearly fell asleep. As she expected, her mother was waiting for her, along with Sammy, who greeted her with a tail wagging with such enthusiasm it shook his entire rear end.

"Lucie, you're exhausted. Oh dear, I was afraid of this."

"I'm okay, Mom."

"Did you eat today?" her mother asked.

"I did," Lucie said, stretching the truth. She had taken the required break but she'd used that time to rest her eyes; just before it was time to return to the kitchen, she'd snatched a roll, slathered it with butter, and called it lunch.

Lucie sat and chatted with her mother for several minutes while giving Sammy attention. Her mother insisted on fixing her some scrambled eggs. Lucie objected but Wendy wouldn't listen, and actually Lucie was glad for the late dinner. Sammy sat obediently at her side.

After Lucie finished her eggs, Wendy laid her head back against the cushioned chair and closed her eyes. "Tell me more about this young man you met."

"Mom, are your blood sugars okay?"

"I'm fine, don't worry about me. I keep a close eye on my insulin levels. Now tell me about Aren."

"I'm not sure what to say . . . just that he's funny

and charming and witty. After the ball dropped we went to an all-night diner and talked nonstop for nearly four hours. He's a writer, and he must be very good because he just got a job with the *New York Gazette*. He has one sister; he's living with her until he can find his own place and he's worried about her."

"Oh?"

"Apparently she broke up with someone she'd been seeing for a couple of years. They had been engaged, but then something went wrong and they called off the wedding and aren't seeing each other any longer. It sounds like Josie is having a hard time of it."

"Aren sounds like an exceptional young man."

"He is." Of that Lucie was certain.

"When will you see him again?" her mother pressed.

"We haven't decided that yet . . . exactly." Lucie didn't want to explain their arrangement, because she knew her wonderful mother would encourage her to meet Aren at the prescribed time and place and wouldn't take no for an answer.

"Did you exchange phone numbers?" Wendy asked.

Lucie shook her head and then realized her mother was resting her eyes. "No, we didn't." She had entertained the idea of asking for Aren's cell number and she felt fairly certain he would want hers, too. But having the necessary contact information might make this decision all the more difficult. This way there was no turning back, no second chances. It was January 7 or nothing.

"He wants me to meet him on the seventh at the top of the Empire State Building," she blurted out, unable to stop herself. Eventually her mother would drag it out of her one way or another.

"Then you should go." Opening her eyes now, Lucie's mother frowned as though confused.

"The thing is, Mom, the timing is all wrong," Lucie whispered.

"So? If you wait until everything is perfect you might lose Aren, and I don't want that to happen."

"I don't either. We decided to give it a week. We'd been up nearly all night and the sparks were there but, like I said, the timing couldn't be worse for me. Aren's starting a new job; I'm already overwhelmed with the restaurant and—"

"My goodness, Lucie Ann, don't you know by now that falling in love is never convenient? I met your father just a short time before he shipped out for the Vietnam War. We had a single day together and then we wrote to each other. Your father wrote the most amazing, beautiful letters."

Lucie had heard the story a thousand times and never tired of it. "A year passed," she continued for her mother.

"Thirteen months. I was in my sophomore year of college and one day out of the blue your father showed up on campus."

"A man in a uniform wasn't exactly the most welcome sight in those days, especially at the university."

"That's putting it mildly."

"But you loved him."

"I did, but I had health issues and I wasn't entirely sure I'd be able to have children."

"And Daddy batted down every objection because he loved you."

"He was determined, all right," Wendy said, her eyes gleaming with the memory.

"And Daddy gave you a deadline."

"Just the way Aren is doing."

"This is different, Mom."

"Not so different, my dear girl. Not so different at all. Like I said, finding the right person doesn't fall into a tidy, neat schedule. You don't turn twenty-one and instantly meet the man of your dreams. It happens when it happens."

Lucie knew that was true from her parents' own love story. Her father had to work hard in order to convince her mother that they should marry. Wendy resisted, and insisted George didn't know what he was getting himself in for. Although the circumstances were different, this was like history repeating itself.

"Promise me you'll meet this young man."

"Mom . . ."

"I know this is what your heart is telling you,

Lucie. You can't fool me, sweetheart. You never could."

That was true. Lucie found deceiving her mother impossible and she disliked it intensely when others deceived her. "Give me time; I've got an entire week to decide."

The morning of January 7, Lucie woke convinced she knew what she wanted. Her mother had worked on her the entire week, talking up the romantic aspect of the meeting. Repeatedly she reminded Lucie of her own starry-eyed courtship with the young army officer who became Lucie's father.

"This afternoon is the date," Wendy casually mentioned over breakfast.

"Yes, Mother, I know."

"Tell me you've decided to meet Aren, because if you don't, I swear I'll go to the Empire State Building to meet him myself."

"Mom."

"Well, okay, I probably wouldn't, but Lucie, I wish you could see how your eyes light up every time you mention him. I felt that way about your father, and, sweetie, we had all those wonderful years together. I want you to find that same happiness."

"I know, Mom . . ."

"Set my mind to rest—just tell me your decision."

Lucie had tried to keep this low-key but clearly

she couldn't. "I'll be there at four and Aren will be waiting for me."

Wendy rubbed her palms together as though it was impossible to contain her joy. "You let that young man know I want to meet him, will you?"

"Of course, Mom. You'll have plenty of opportunity to meet Aren."

Lucie loved her mother's enthusiasm.

"I've arranged to get off work early," Lucie explained. "I'll take the subway into the city."

"Perfect. You'll call once you're there, won't you? I refuse to be left in the dark. I want to know what happens when he sees you, okay?"

"Give me a few minutes to at least greet him." She'd phone after that kiss Aren had promised her. Lucie had trouble holding back a smile. After all, it'd all started with a simple kiss. Well, in truth, it hadn't been that simple. Things rarely were.

Lucie had never been a clock watcher, especially on the job. That day, however, her gaze bounced against the wall several times as she counted the hours away. At three o'clock, a full hour before the scheduled rendezvous, Lucie changed clothes, refreshed her makeup, and headed out the door to the subway station. She was just about to descend the stairwell when her cellphone rang.

"Is this Lucie Ferrara?" a woman's voice asked.

"Yes."

"This is New York Methodist Hospital. We have

your mother here. She took a bad spill and broke her arm. I'm afraid she's going to need surgery . . ."

"Oh dear. Is Mom all right? She's diabetic."

"Not to worry, her blood sugars are stabilized."

Lucie grimaced at the thought of her mother in pain. "I'll be right there," Lucie said, doing her best to control the sense of panic she felt. She paused at the top of the stairwell and looked out at the city. The view of the Empire State Building showed in the background. There was no help for it now. No way would she be able to make the appointment with Aren. Disappointment settled into the pit of her stomach. This was divine intervention. Despite her decision he'd be there waiting for her . . . and she wasn't going to show.

Lucie was at her mother's bedside when Wendy woke following the surgery. Her mother blinked at Lucie and then frowned.

"You met Aren, didn't you?"

Rather than respond verbally, she shook her head.

"I told the hospital not to call you."

"Mom, I needed to be here to talk to the doctors. What happened?" Lucie already knew. Her mother's blood sugar had dropped again and she'd fallen. Thankfully she was within sight of a neighbor lady who immediately called 911.

"Oh, Lucie, I feel so bad for you. This is all my fault."

"Mom, it wasn't meant to be."

"No, no, I don't believe it. I just don't believe it." Her mother tightly squeezed her eyes shut and her lips started to move.

"What are you doing?" Lucie asked.

"Sh-h, I'm praying."

"Praying for what?" Lucie teased.

"You and Aren. I'm asking God to bring you two together again in His timing. He's going to do it, you know. Trust me. God is going to work this out because He knows I'll never forgive myself if you lost out on meeting the love of your life because of me."

"That's very sweet, Mom, but I believe God's got more important prayers to answer than this."

Wendy scoffed. "Don't be a silly goose. And don't be surprised if you and Aren cross paths within the next few days. Mark my words on that. Mark my words."

"Yes, Mom." Although Lucie agreed, on the inside she had a storehouse of reservations that Almighty God really cared about something as minor as this. And at the same time she couldn't keep from hoping He did.

Chapter Four

December
Eleven Months Later

Gabriel opened the huge book of prayers and scanned through the large number of requests that crossed his desk on an hourly basis. He issued orders to the Prayer Ambassadors left and right. Heaven was abuzz with activity.

They were coming upon the Christmas season, which was often their busiest time of year, stretching the angels assigned as Prayer Ambassadors to their limit. Earth was hectic at this time of year; humans were harried and Gabriel wanted to stay ahead of the rush as much as possible.

He ran his finger down the lengthy list and paused when he found one that remained unanswered from a New York woman named Wendy Ferrara. It was almost eleven months old. He frowned and then tapped his foot. Something tugged at his mind, a nagging sensation that he hadn't been able to put to rest.

Ah, he remembered this prayer. Upon receiving it, he'd ordered an investigation. Once the report was back, he'd read it, grumbled under his breath, and then set it aside until he could decide the best way to handle this awkward situation. Apparently his three favorite angels had taken matters into their own hands. And worse, they had dragged their young apprentice into it, too. Gabriel had assigned Shirley, Goodness, and Mercy as mentors to Will, and they'd done an excellent job. Well, other than this one not-so-minor indiscretion. This was a delicate matter that required careful handling.

The time to deal with Wendy Ferrara's prayer was now. He called for the three Prayer Ambassadors and their apprentice. No sooner had he sent for them when Shirley, Goodness, and Mercy appeared, their wings fluttering with excitement and anticipation.

Taking on a serious pose, Gabriel looked up from his desk. The three were all smiles.

"You asked to see us," Shirley said, looking serene and sublime. These angels were magnificent creatures. Some of God's finest work, along with the Warrior Angels and, naturally, humans, who were created in God's own image.

"I know why you sent for us," Goodness bragged.

Gabriel arched his thick white brows. "You do?"

"You're ready to give us an assignment on Earth."

Mercy nodded eagerly. "You've already run low on Prayer Ambassadors and are looking to put us back in action. Our methods might not be conventional, but we get prayers answered."

Gabriel didn't respond as he made a show of turning the page of the prayer request book. "Actually this has to do with—"

"Sorry I'm late. I was . . ." Will popped in, and seeing Gabriel with his three mentors, he stopped short.

"I'm pleased you could join us," Gabriel said with just a hint of sarcasm. He quite liked the lad and felt Will would serve God well once he was properly trained.

"I'm glad, too." Will straightened to full attention, folding his wings tightly against his body, and stood with his back straight, his look respectful.

Gabriel stepped around his desk and clasped his hands behind him. "It's come to my attention that the four of you made an unscheduled visit to Earth last January."

"New Year's Eve, to be precise," Shirley supplied and raised her index finger. "I want it on the record that I was against the idea from the beginning. I wanted no part of this scheme, and—"

"But you joined in," Gabriel said, cutting her off.

"Well, yes, I realize it probably looks bad but I felt having someone sensible tag along was absolutely necessary. There was no telling what trouble Goodness and Mercy could get into without me there to watch over them."

"We didn't—"

Gabriel cut Goodness off. "I want to know who was responsible for the fiasco involving Lucie Ferrara and Aren Fairchild?"

Shirley, Goodness, and Mercy all found it necessary to look elsewhere with their lips tightly pinched together.

"That would be me," Will murmured. He, too, had trouble meeting Gabriel's gaze.

"Explain what happened." Gabriel used his sternest voice.

Will stepped forward and stared straight ahead. "To be fair to my mentors I was warned not to get involved with humans, but I—"

"You mean to say you actually mingled with humans?"

Will's slow nod revealed his reluctance. "Mercy explained only those with spiritual eyes could see us."

"Did anyone notice you?"

"No."

"You're sure?" Gabriel pressed.

"Not entirely, but if I was recognized no one said anything."

Gabriel walked around his desk. "You'd best tell me everything." His gaze connected with Mercy, who sighed and moved to stand with Will. "I accept responsibility. I lost sight of Shirley and while I was searching for her, Will disappeared."

"In other words this trouble is a direct result of your disobedience." He pinned her with his eyes.

He was silently pleased she was willing to step forward and admit her mistake, although he had a sneaky suspicion all three were involved in this debacle.

Mercy squirmed uncomfortably under his intense scrutiny. "I'd like to think of our short sojourn to Earth as an unplanned training exercise."

Gabriel directed his next question to Will. "And what did you learn, young man?"

"Ah . . ." Will seemed to go speechless and looked to his mentors for help.

"Well, for one thing," Shirley said, coming to her charge's rescue, "I learned not to allow cranky toddlers to distract me."

"And then Goodness got lured away by those network cameras and I had to distract her before she showed up on the Jumbotron again . . ."

"And that's when the bell struck midnight and all those humans started kissing and singing," Will chimed in.

"And . . ." Gabriel wanted the full story.

"And I introduced these two people," the apprentice angel admitted, looking down at his feet.

"Lucie and Aren?"

"I didn't get their names."

"Lucie and Aren," Gabriel said a bit louder.

"They kissed," Will said excitedly. "I saw them."

"And you interfered with God's plan for them to meet," Gabriel muttered, shaking his head as though thoroughly discouraged.

"You mean God intended for them to meet all along?" Mercy asked, her voice slightly elevated with excitement.

"Yes, but their meeting wasn't scheduled to happen for several months and now everything is askew."

"Is there anything I can do to set matters right?" Will asked. "Because I'd be willing to volunteer to return to Earth and do whatever is necessary to make amends."

I just bet you would, Gabriel thought. It was already apparent that Will had caught the enthusiasm for Earth as badly as his mentors.

"That is," Will continued, "if you were willing to trust me again."

To his credit the apprentice looked appropriately chagrined and repentant. Gabriel mused over the question as he rubbed his chin, wondering if there was a simple way around this problem. "Well, with some effort you might be able to untangle this mess."

"Does this mean it'll be necessary to return to Earth?" Goodness asked breathlessly, hopefully.

"And naturally as Will's mentors we would need to accompany him," Shirley added as though it was understood Will couldn't possibly handle this awkward situation without their assistance.

"Well . . ."

"At great personal sacrifice, I'll personally volunteer to accompany Will without the others," Mercy offered.

Gabriel watched as Mercy's two friends glared at

her in undisguised outrage. Several feathers broke loose and floated to the floor, a sure indication that they were perturbed by Mercy's willingness to leave them behind.

"Seeing that the three of you were in this together I feel it's only fair that you all accompany Will and straighten this out."

"We'll leave right this minute." Shirley didn't bother to disguise her zeal to take on the project.

"Hold on," Gabriel said, stopping them. "There have been a number of significant changes."

"Oh."

"In order for you to understand the complexity of the situation, you'll need to take a look at Lucie's and Aren's lives now, all these months later."

He waved his arms and the thin veil that separated Earth from heaven's view vanished. The three Prayer Ambassadors along with their apprentice intently watched through the clearing fog.

"What's that?" Will asked.

"That's Heavenly Delights," Gabriel said. "Lucie and her mother opened the restaurant in April. It's doing amazingly well. Lucie creates tantalizing desserts, and the restaurant has caused quite a stir in Brooklyn—and all without printed advertisement. Their success has come by word of mouth." He wondered if any of them got his small pun. Apparently not.

"That's wonderful."

"Lucie puts in long hours. Her mother serves as

the hostess. Wendy is warm and welcoming and makes their dinner guests feel as if they were coming into her home."

"Heavenly Delights," Goodness repeated. "What a perfect name for a restaurant."

"Most everyone assumes the name comes from the wonderful desserts, which are said to be inspired," Gabriel explained.

"You mean it doesn't?"

"No." He was quite pleased that the idea for the name had come from someone they all knew quite well. "Actually, another angel, a dear, dear friend of mine, happened to give it that name."

"What friend?"

"I realize it must come as a surprise but amazingly I do have friends."

"Of course . . ."

"Naturally."

"It was Mrs. Miracle," Gabriel said, grinning. "Because of Emily, Lucie got a last-minute catering contract just before Christmas a couple of years back. That event is what got the ball rolling with the restaurant."

"And now the restaurant is a reality."

"What's that in the corner?" Will pointed to the refrigeration display unit close to the hostess table.

"That," Gabriel said, "is a display case for Lucie's sweet concoctions. Her desserts have become so popular that it's difficult to get a reservation for dinner. Wendy—that's her mother—came up with the idea of selling the desserts as a take-out item. The idea has worked exceptionally well."

"When were Aren and Lucie scheduled to meet . . . originally?" Will wanted to know.

"In just a few days, Earth time."

"How?"

"Well, they were never supposed to bump into each other, if that's what you're asking."

Will did look wretched over all this. "I'd like to do what I can to make matters right."

"And I'll give you the opportunity."

"Thank you, Gabriel."

"Yes, thank you," Shirley, Goodness, and Mercy echoed.

Gabriel sighed. He hoped he wouldn't come to regret this decision. "Aren Fairchild works for the *New York Gazette* as the food critic who writes under the pseudonym of Eaton Well, which is a name owned by the newspaper."

"Eaton Well," Mercy repeated. "That's clever."

"He's under contract not to reveal his identity. The Lifestyle editor finds up-and-coming restaurants for Aren."

"Then he makes a reservation, dines there, and writes up a review without anyone at the restaurant knowing who their secret customer is," Mercy said, thinking out loud.

"Exactly."

Will looked crestfallen. "They were originally scheduled to meet at the restaurant, when Aren falls in love with the woman behind the fabulous desserts."

"Not all matters like this go as planned." Gabriel didn't want to break the young man's spirit. His heart was in the right place.

"What's happening now?" Mercy asked, peering down into the kitchen.

"Let's find out," Gabriel said. With a wave of his arms, the conversation between Lucie and her mother suddenly became audible.

"Lucie," Wendy said, stepping into the pantry.

Lucie sat on a crate of recently delivered supplies with a copy of the *New York Gazette* spread open. The instant she heard her mother's voice, Lucie tried unsuccessfully to hide the newspaper.

Her mother paused and her shoulders sagged. "Oh, Lucie, you're looking for Aren's name again, aren't you?"

Lucie couldn't see any reason to hide the obvious. "It isn't here. He must not have taken the job after all."

Her mother's smile faded. "I hate that I was responsible for you not meeting him that day. I can barely look at the Empire State Building and not think about the missed opportunity."

"Mom, stop. It wasn't meant to be." She'd told herself that a hundred times and tried to believe it, although she hadn't been able to get Aren out of her mind.

"But you still think of him."

Lucie didn't bother to deny it. She did think of Aren. As hard as she tried to forget him, it hadn't worked. She couldn't help wondering how long he'd waited for her that day. Had he stood in the cold, hoping she'd arrive with a logical explanation of why she was late? Did he regret that they hadn't exchanged contact information the way she did? "If it's meant to happen we'll meet again." She remembered her mother's prayer and added one of her own.

"I came in to tell you every table is booked again tonight and we're already getting reservation requests into the new year."

"That's wonderful."

"I'd like for you to take New Year's Eve off this year."

"Mom, I can't do that. It's bound to be one of the busiest nights of the season for us."

"Don't worry . . . we'll bring in extra help."

"Mom, I can't. I know what you're thinking. You want me to return to Times Square on the off chance I'll run into Aren again. I can't do that. I won't. It would be nothing more than a wild-goose chase, an impossibility."

"Oh, Lucie, I didn't realize you could be this stubborn."

Lucie laughed. She couldn't help it. "And just who do you think I inherited this trait from?"

"Your father," Wendy insisted and then they both laughed.

"I'm pleased to see how well the restaurant is doing," Shirley said.

"Poor Lucie, though," Will whispered and exhaled sharply. "She's never forgotten Aren."

"What was all that talk about a meeting?" Goodness scratched the side of her head as if she'd missed something important.

Gabriel explained.

"Lucie didn't show?" Mercy inquired anxiously.

"No, and Aren waited as long as the guards would let him. He returned a second time as well."

"Oh my, poor Aren."

"Does he think of Lucie, too?"

Gabriel nodded. "All the time."

"Just a minute . . . hold on here." Mercy started pacing Gabriel's office.

"What?" Shirley asked, studying her friend.

"What are we waiting for?" Goodness looked from Mercy to Gabriel. "We have work to do."

Mercy started waving her hand, one wing flapping as she spoke. "I get it. I get it. Aren's a food critic. His byline will never show in the paper in order to keep his identity a secret."

"Yes," Gabriel said and waited for Mercy to complete her thought.

"And he's been assigned to review Heavenly Delights, right?"

"Right."

"And that's how they were originally intended to meet?"

Gabriel said nothing. He wanted them to work this out for themselves.

"He couldn't let her know about the pseudonym," Shirley reminded them, "because of his contract with the newspaper."

"But he would fall in love with Lucie's desserts even before he met her," Mercy cried with what appeared to be perfect logic.

"Now it's our job to be sure Aren and Lucie meet again." Will's face brightened with excitement. "We can do that, Gabriel, leave everything to us."

"You're sure you're up to the task?"

"Without question."

"Then have at it, my friends. And this time make sure you stay on task."

"Not a problem," Mercy promised.

Before he could issue a warning, the four disappeared. Gabriel grinned and then shook his head. All he could do now was stand back and watch as these four headed for Earth.

Heaven help them all.

Literally.

Chapter Five

"Look, Aren's already at the restaurant," Will whispered. Shirley, Goodness, and Mercy joined him and the four gazed down from the light fixtures in the restaurant Heavenly Delights.

"Is that Lucie's mother?" Goodness asked, looking toward the middle-aged woman who greeted Aren.

"Which woman? There are several."

"The one who's leading him to his table."

"That's her."

"Who's that woman with Aren?"

Will shook his head. "I don't have a clue. She wasn't with him on New Year's Eve. In fact I've never seen her before. Have any of you?"

No one seemed to know. Mercy sighed, worried now. Perhaps Aren had met another woman, someone he liked even better than Lucie. The two certainly looked to be chummy, laughing and joking with each other. Oh dear, that would pose a significant problem. Something would need to be done and quickly.

Will wrung his hands, apparently worried as well. "Do you think it might be too late? Do you think Aren's found someone else?"

"It could be a colleague."

"Or a friend," Shirley suggested.

"S-h-h, let's listen to their conversation. Maybe that will tell us what we need to know." Mercy didn't understand why she had to be the practical one in the group. The others were far too quick to leap to conclusions.

"First impressions of a restaurant are important," Aren said, unfolding the linen napkin and spreading it across his lap, looking up at his sister. "What are your thoughts?"

Josie looked around her, apparently taking in the ambience of the room. "The decorations are simple and subtle. I like that."

"I do, too," Aren agreed. Eye appeal was important—the dining experience was never just about the quality of the food.

"What about the hostess?" he asked next. His sister had dined with him several times and he'd come to appreciate her input. Tonight's dinner was especially important. He'd worked for the newspaper nearly a year now and reviewed many different types of restaurants, from the very expensive to the very cheap, from the most famous and established to undiscovered holes in the wall. But he felt that a new, up-and-coming place like Heavenly Delights provided the greatest opportunity for both his readers and the restaurant.

Josie smiled. "She sort of reminds me of Aunt Lucille, so warm and friendly." She paused and stared at him. "You're frowning again. Any time I mention Aunt Lucille lately you get this funny look."

"Do not."

"Do, too. I'm your sister and I know a frown on you when I see one. You're thinking about that girl you met New Year's Eve again, aren't you? Her name was Lucie."

"No." His denial was adamant. "Besides, I asked you not to bring her up again." He'd made his case, given Lucie time, and apparently she wasn't interested. Nothing gained, nothing lost . . . although Aren hadn't been able to put her out of his mind.

Josie simply shook her head, Aren noted, indicating she didn't think it was worth squabbling about. If they were going to argue about anything it should be Josie and her nonrelationship with Jack. His sister did a good job of hiding her broken heart but Aren wasn't fooled. She was miserable and far too proud to admit it. He didn't understand how two people who loved each other to the point of getting close to exchanging vows would suddenly decide to call it quits. Apparently, as the time for the wedding drew close, they'd both gotten cold feet. They'd argued and now stubbornness had taken over common sense.

"Are we going to bicker or look at the menu?" Josie asked, opening the menu. "What looks good to you?"

"I'm in the mood for fish." Aren scanned the seafood section and found it diverse and impressive. The Dover sole served with beurre blanc sauce appealed to him. "That sauce can be tricky and is a good test of a chef's expertise." So was seafood, which so many restaurants tended to overcook.

"Did you hear that?" Will said triumphantly. "The woman with Aren is his sister."

"And he's still thinking about Lucie." This was going to work out better than they'd planned. Mercy could see it already. She watched as brother and sister bantered back and forth, obviously good friends as well as siblings. After a few minutes, she glanced around and discovered Will was nowhere in sight.

"Where's Will?" Shirley asked.

"I'm here," he said, returning from some unknown destination. Mercy felt it was necessary to explain that it was important that they all stay together, and when she finished she discovered Shirley had disappeared as well.

"Now where's Shirley?"

"The waitress is friendly and helpful," Aren told his sister. Heavenly Delights was turning out to be everything it promised. If the food was as good as reported, he would gladly write up a favorable review. To this point he found it to be a pleasant dining experience, but the true test, as with every restaurant, was the food.

Several people had contacted the newspaper about this up-and-coming restaurant that had captured the attention of Brooklyn diners. The number of recommendations had been impressive enough for the editor to put it at the top of the list. But in Aren's experience, many restaurants that came highly touted often didn't live up to the hype. It was his job to notice the details most diners overlooked. It was like a singer who was gifted with perfect pitch. To anyone else a performer might sound fabulous, but someone with a good ear would instantly recognize when a note was even the slightest bit off key. Aren felt he had "perfect pitch" when it came to restaurants and food.

To this point everything met with his satisfaction. The restaurant was clean. The staff efficient without being intrusive, repeating the specials of the day without needing to refer to notes. Their wine order was taken and water glasses were promptly filled. A few minutes after their wine was served, freshly baked bread, still warm from the oven, was delivered to their table. Almost as soon as they set their menus aside their server came for their order. Ah, yes, this restaurant did show promise.

Aren and his sister sipped their wine and after

just the right amount of time their meal arrived. His sole was artfully arranged on the plate with small dollops of whipped potatoes in golden toasted swirls. The vegetable was roasted asparagus topped with lemon zest.

"Oh my, that does look delicious." His sister eyed his plate appreciatively.

"Yours does, too." Josie had ordered the chicken Parmesan. The chicken had been fried to a lovely brown and topped with a blend of Italian cheeses. The meal was served with a side of spaghetti covered in a rich, red marinara sauce. Her dinner included both a side salad and toasted garlic bread. The scent of the warm bread and garlic was like an aphrodisiac. It was far too easy to overdo the garlic. The kitchen hadn't.

"My compliments to the chef." Josie reached for her fork.

"You haven't tasted your dinner yet," he chastised.

"Well, my goodness, if it tastes even half as good as it smells, I'll be in heaven."

Aren grinned and rolled his eyes. Looks could be deceiving.

"Speaking of the chef."

Aren raised his hand, stopping her. "Don't mention the name."

Josie set her fork aside. "Why not?"

"It's better I not know, otherwise it might influence my opinion. I've seen too many others in my line of work be influenced by a cooking celebrity." He didn't dare say anything that would indicate to anyone within hearing distance that he wrote for the *Gazette*. Aren judged the food. Not the reputation. Not the number of cookbooks published and certainly not the fame. What mattered to him was the food and the overall dining experience.

"You haven't tasted your dinner yet," Josie said.

Filled with anticipation, Aren reached for his fork. The sole was cooked perfectly. His mouth watered with eagerness to sample his first bite. He closed his eyes, expecting sheer delight.

Delight wasn't the word he'd use to describe the sole. In fact, it took restraint not to spit it out. Only by sheer willpower did he manage to swallow his food.

In a word the sole was *dreadful*. The beurre blanc sauce was salty to the point that it ruined the entire dish. Apparently the chef realized the mistake and overcompensated with lemon, which left an acidic flavor so powerful he nearly puckered his lips. If that wasn't bad enough, he distinctly tasted cayenne pepper. The only thing he considered edible was the asparagus, which was cooked to perfection. Unfortunately, everything else on his plate wasn't fit for human consumption.

This meal was a serious disappointment. By contrast his sister seemed to savor every bite.

"Is something wrong with your dinner, sir?" the waitperson asked as she removed Josie's empty plate.

Unable to force himself to swallow a second bite of the fish, Aren's plate remained basically untouched except for the one bite of sole, potatoes, and asparagus. Even the potatoes were off, so heavily buttered that their natural flavor was lost.

"No, everything is fine." Aren forced himself to smile. In other circumstances he would have returned the plate to the kitchen and refused to pay.

"Could I interest you in dessert?" the waiter asked. "We've got a reputation for our wonderful desserts. I highly recommend our sea salt caramel mousse."

"Salted mousse?" Aren repeated. Apparently the chef had a love affair with the salt shaker. Frankly he'd had all he could take. Nothing sweet would redeem this restaurant. He'd already gone through one glass of wine and two glasses of water in an effort to remove the foul taste from his mouth.

"I will," Josie volunteered, far too eagerly, in his opinion.

"I'll take a bite of hers," Aren said.

His sister ordered the mousse and to be completely fair, Aren gave it a taste and it wasn't half bad. He'd sampled others that were comparable but this chef way overdid the salt. This could be a health hazard to diners with high blood pressure or on a low-salt diet. The menu should come with a warning, which he planned to mention in his review.

"Aren didn't like his dinner," Will moaned.

"You don't know that."

Goodness was such an optimist. Even Mercy could see that Aren hadn't taken more than one small bite of the fish. He'd scrunched up his face as if he'd bitten into a lemon and hardly tasted anything else afterward. He'd returned his plate to the kitchen practically untouched.

"His sister ate her dinner."

A suspicion began to brew in Mercy's mind. Each one of her friends had disappeared for short amounts of time. Could it be . . . was it possible . . . ? Surely they wouldn't tamper with the food.

"It wasn't supposed to happen like this." Will was more than a little upset and continued to rub his palms together as he mulled over the situation.

"Will, you vanished for a few moments just after Aren ordered the sole."

"Hmmm, yeah."

"Can you tell me where you went?"

"Ah . . ."

"You visited the kitchen, didn't you?"

"Ah . . ."

Enough said, that was exactly what Will had done. "You didn't by chance happen to add a bit of salt to the beurre blanc sauce, did you?"

Will shrugged and then reluctantly admitted to the deed. "Perhaps a little, but just a few shakes. All I was looking to do was heighten the natural flavors."

"You added salt?" Shirley cried, tossing her hands into the air. "How could you?"

"I was only trying to help," Will muttered.

"I fear Will wasn't the only one," Goodness confessed. "I added a little extra lemon."

Almost afraid to ask, Mercy looked to Shirley.

"Seeing that red spice, I thought to brighten up the dish a bit," the former Guardian Angel admitted. "And while I was there I might have stirred in a bit of this and that."

"Oh dear." Mercy's shoulders sank. This was even worse than she'd assumed.

"What about you?" Will asked.

Mercy exhaled slowly and admitted she'd taken part in this, too. "Guilty as charged."

"We all added extra spice to that wonderful sauce." Will started to wring his hands. "We've ruined everything. Aren won't have any choice but to write a scathing review. People will read it; it won't be just the printed version either. Aren's review will go online and soon it'll be all over the Internet."

"Lucie and her mother will be ruined," Goodness cried. "Their business will go down in flames. Wendy's entire life's savings will dwindle away bit by bit and the two of them will lose everything. They won't be able to pay their bills and will end up living on the streets, homeless and alone, and it will be my fault."

"And mine," Shirley wailed.

"We've ruined their lives." Goodness was close to tears.

Mercy waved her arms, silencing her friends. "We have bigger worries than what's going to happen to Lucie and her mother."

"You mean there's more?" Will cried.

"You mean it gets worse?"

With profound sadness Mercy nodded. "Much worse."

Goodness cupped her mouth. "What more could happen?"

Mercy didn't hold back. "Gabriel is going to find out what we did."

Her two friends and Will gasped in horror.

"We've really done it this time. Moving a few aircraft carriers around is nothing compared to tampering with Lucie's sauce."

"This is the end for sure," Shirley wailed.

"Did I hear one of you mention my name?" All at once Gabriel stood before them. He'd never looked more daunting, or unapproachable. His massive arms were crossed over his chest as he frowned down upon them.

Will scooted closer to Mercy. Shirley and Goodness crowded her sides as the four made themselves as small as possible.

"What happened here?" he demanded.

No one spoke.

"I asked you a question." His voice seemed to boom and ricochet around the restaurant. It was a wonder no human heard him, although the walls felt as if they'd buckled with the power of his words.

"We tried to help Lucie impress Aren." Mercy's voice sounded as if she'd been tossed into a deep well. It echoed in her ears high-pitched and tinny.

"By adding salt, lemon, and cayenne to the sauce and a bit of extra butter to the potatoes?"

So he already knew.

"I'm afraid so."

"What can we do to make this right?" Will asked. The dear boy really was concerned.

"It's too late for that. Aren is going to write a review that isn't the least bit favorable." Gabriel didn't pull any punches.

"Will it affect their business?"

"It will have the potential to destroy this restaurant. The *New York Gazette* can do that, you know."

"Oh, no," Goodness groaned. She had such a tender heart. Mercy knew that her friend would never forgive herself if Lucie and her mother lost the restaurant because of what they'd done.

"We were only trying to help," Shirley said. "Please tell me that we can go back and undo what just happened."

Sadness rimmed Gabriel's eyes. "You know you can't."

"But in heaven . . ."

"This is Earth and we are bound by the frailties

of a fallen world. There's no undo button, no delete key. It is what it is."

"What's going to happen?" Mercy pleaded. Gabriel had the gift of being able to look into the future. Unfortunately, that was a skill they didn't possess.

Gabriel sadly shook his head. "I think it might be best to wait and let you discover this for yourself. The four of you broke one of the cardinal rules of being Prayer Ambassadors."

"We stepped in to help," Goodness confessed.

"Our role is to guide."

"We have a hands-off directive."

"Now you will see for yourself what happens when you overstep in giving aid to humans."

"But our intentions were good."

"Intentions," Gabriel repeated. "Intentions, my young man, are pavement along the road to destruction."

"But—"

"This will be a painful lesson for you all."

Mercy dreaded what was sure to happen next. "We're banished from Earth, aren't we?" Never again would they be allowed to visit humans. They might even lose their status as Prayer Ambassadors and be stripped of their wings. The thought was almost more than she could bear to consider.

Gabriel's gaze focused on the four. "Have you learned your lesson?"

All four nodded simultaneously.

"Can you promise not to interfere in human affairs again?"

"I promise," Will lamented. "I'll never add salt to another dish as long as I serve the Lord."

"Shirley, Goodness, and Mercy." Gabriel turned his attention to the three of them. "You know better."

They hung their heads, their wings drooping so that the tips brushed against the floor.

"What about Aren and Lucie?" Mercy felt she had to know how best to help these two . . . guide them, that is. She and her colleagues were responsible for messing up God's plan. The least they could do was make things right, if possible.

"Ah, yes," Gabriel mused aloud. "Aren and Lucie. Well, my friends, we'll just have to wait and see what happens next."

Chapter Six

Horrified by the review of Heavenly Delights in the *New York Gazette,* Lucie crunched up the newspaper and then immediately stomped on it. She'd read it multiple times, searching for a glimmer of something positive. Anything that could be considered constructive, but there was nothing. An encouraging word simply wasn't to be found. The restaurant had been panned by Eaton Well. The review had been scathing, sarcastic, and that was only the first paragraph. It got worse from that point on. This review was disastrous and had the potential to ruin them.

"Sweetheart, are you reading it again?" her mother asked.

Lucie slammed her foot down on the crumpled-up newspaper and ground it back and forth as if putting out a cigarette butt. This was what she'd like to do to the reviewer, squish him like the roach he was. The man or woman was a parasite. A bug that needed to be exterminated. Eaton Well had been completely unfair, mocking her food, belittling her talent, and even going so far as to suggest she give up cooking entirely.

"Lucie, Lucie, sweetie, let it go." Wendy placed a restraining hand on her daughter's arm. "Don't let that ridiculous article upset you so much."

Her mother remained cool and calm, which served only to infuriate Lucie more. Apparently her gentle-hearted, optimistic mother didn't understand what this might do to their restaurant. This could be the beginning of the end.

Wendy seemed to take this horrible review in her stride, whereas Lucie was at the boiling point, but then she'd been the brunt of much of the printed piece.

"You're taking this much too seriously," Wendy warned.

Lucie stared at her mother. Wendy had always been the optimist in the family, the one who never failed to find something good in any situation. When her mother had first read the review, Wendy had actually suggested that the reviewer must have had a bad day. The poor reporter was probably on a deadline and hadn't taken time to enjoy his meal.

"Don't you understand that a review like this could ruin us?" If Lucie had said it once, she'd said it ten times, but apparently the words had yet to sink into her mother's head.

"Perhaps so, but personally I don't think we need to worry." Wendy poured hot tea into her cup and blew onto the steaming liquid before she took a sip.

"We haven't seen a decline in reservations, have we?"

"How could we?" Lucie snapped. "The review is less than twenty-four hours old. Mom, don't you understand? Readers pay attention to these restaurant reviews. Even if we manage to survive, this has the potential to set us back for years." Lucie didn't want to be negative, but one of them had to be realistic. To be reviewed in its own right was a big deal. With literally thousands of restaurants to choose from, to have Eaton Well dine at their establishment meant Heavenly Delights had caused something of a stir. Enough to warrant the *Gazette*'s attention.

Still, how dare the reviewer criticize her sauce. She'd worked hard on that recipe and she'd put it up against any chef's in the industry.

Wendy remained unfazed. "Lucie, you worry too much. We have a large number of loyal customers."

"Don't you understand? Didn't you read the article?" Lucie didn't need to retrieve the printed page. After reading the worst of it several times over she had the comments memorized: "*Heavenly Delights is anything but. Those with high blood pressure beware, the chef has a heavy hand with both lemon and salt. So much salt that they must have drained the Dead Sea for the beurre blanc sauce . . . seriously, whoever is in the kitchen needs to return to culinary school or hang up their hat entirely.*" Lucie was too upset to continue.

"I agree that comment wasn't the least bit kind."

"It was a desperate effort to sound clever and witty at my expense." Lucie seethed every time she thought about those cutting remarks.

"I don't think you should take it personally, Lucie."

"Not take it personally! How can you say that? This is definitely personal. It's an attack on my credibility. The reviewer might as well have said I'm unqualified. Come to think of it, that's in the article as well." Lucie struggled to contain her outrage. Of all the nerve. Eaton Well knew nothing about her, nor was it necessary to write his or her review. The food critic didn't have a clue of the sacrifices she'd made in order to attend culinary school or how she'd worked nights and weekends until she was too exhausted to think. As far as she was concerned this critic was heartless and unfair.

Her mother continued to drink her tea, setting the cup carefully back in the saucer. "Answer me this: When was the last time you took a night off?"

Lucie collapsed into the chair. "Are you suggesting that I'm so overworked that I—"

"I'm not saying anything of the sort. What I am suggesting is that you need to step back, take a deep breath, and let this roll off your back. A single bad review isn't going to destroy us."

Lucie wished she could believe that. Clearly her mother didn't have a clue how serious this situation was. Until recently Wendy hadn't been part of the culinary world. Lucie's mother didn't understand that these restaurant reviews could be incredibly influential.

The phone rang and Wendy reached across the kitchen counter and snagged it.

Lucie only half-listened to the conversation. It didn't take long for her to recognize that the person on the other end of the line was a friend of her mother's who'd phoned to commiserate.

"I'm not the least bit concerned," Wendy insisted. "I know my daughter. Anyone who's ever tasted Lucie's cooking recognizes that she's a fully qualified chef. My daughter knows her way around the kitchen. No, no, we aren't going to file charges against the newspaper. This was one person's opinion. Most people prefer to judge a restaurant themselves. It's unfortunate that he or she had a bad experience but we can't make everyone happy all the time."

That was true enough, Lucie realized. Still, she would have preferred to have this reporter brag endlessly about her cooking instead of lambasting her on every level.

Wendy had no sooner hung up the phone when it rang a second time. "Oh, hi, Juliana. Yes, of course we saw it. No, I'm not worried. Thank you. I'll tell Lucie. Really?" After a couple of moments of silence, her mother sat up straighter and fixed her gaze on Lucie.

Lucie couldn't help but notice the way her mother's eyes brightened.

"Of course I'll tell her. This is just wonderful. Thanks so much, Juliana. You've made my day." Wearing a huge smile, her mother docked the phone.

"What did Juliana say?" Lucie couldn't help being curious at the change in her mother's posture.

"Juliana went on the newspaper's website. She always was one to keep up with technology. All that social media techie stuff is beyond me."

"And?" Lucie pressed.

"Well, apparently several people have taken exception to the review and have left comments."

"Really. Several people? Did she mention a number?"

Wendy nodded. "She said you should check it out yourself and you'd be impressed. I believe she said there were already three hundred comments, all disagreeing with the review."

"Three hundred." Lucie felt like dancing around the room.

"And not a single one of them is related to this family," Wendy boasted.

Lucie immediately sat down at her desk, which she'd set up in the corner of their cozy living room. Sammy, who sensed something was wrong, waddled over and sat down at her feet, resting his chin on her foot as though to comfort her.

Lucie booted up her computer, logged onto the Internet, and went to the home page for the newspaper. Sure enough, the Heavenly Delights review dominated the comments directed at the newspaper. Lucie could barely believe her eyes. Her hand covered her mouth as she read comment after comment praising the restaurant. Several people mentioned Lucie's signature dishes and nearly everyone raved about the desserts. Wendy was right. Their loyal customers hadn't remained silent. They'd come to the restaurant's defense in droves. It was barely noon and the comments already numbered over three hundred.

"Take that, Eaton Well," Lucie murmured, grinning uncontrollably.

"What did I tell you," Wendy said, coming to stand behind her. "We don't have a thing to worry about."

Lucie desperately wanted to believe that.

A summons from the managing editor wasn't unusual, but it was the way the message came to Aren. He'd been asked to stop by the editor's desk *at his earliest convenience*.

Sandy Markus had been with the paper nearly thirty years. She was a pro and didn't stand on ceremony, nor was she shy about sharing her opinion. The woman had grit and guts—both necessary to rise this high in what was once considered a man's world. Sandy had not only broken the mold; she'd helped shape a new one. Aren respected and liked his boss even though she had the power to intimidate him.

When Aren appeared at her office door, Sandy glanced up and motioned him inside.

"Close the door," she instructed.

Aren reluctantly complied with her request. If Sandy wanted the door closed, it usually meant bad news.

Aren's stomach sank.

The managing editor continued to focus on her computer screen. "Have a seat," she instructed. She wasn't the stereotypical newswoman. Sandy was tall and thin, with short, wiry hair that she groomed into submission with mousse until it stood straight up on end. In her mid-sixties, her face had weathered well through the years.

"Is there a problem?" Aren asked. As far as he knew his work had been more than satisfactory.

Aren didn't expect Sandy to praise his writing. She'd let it be known she expected his articles to be of top quality. If they weren't he could seek employment elsewhere.

Aren took a seat. "What's this about?" He hated being called to task when he didn't have any idea what he'd done wrong.

"Heavenly Delights," she muttered, reluctantly tearing her gaze away from the monitor. She removed her eyeglasses and a deep frown marred her brow as she studied him. "You wrote the review of the restaurant, right?"

"I did." Aren stood by his piece. The food had been some of the worst in his experience. As far as he was concerned, whoever was doing the cooking had a lot to learn. The chicken dish was satisfactory, but that showed no real expertise. The true test had been the sole and sauce, and in that the chef had failed miserably.

"You were scathing in your remarks."

Scathing wasn't the word he'd use. "I was honest."

Sandy glared back at him from the other side of her desk. "Apparently your review has caused quite a stir."

He laughed. "It has?" He couldn't imagine why, other than the obvious fact that the restaurant needed a new chef.

"I don't suppose you've taken a look at the website or the Facebook page? There are hundreds of rebuttals to your review between the two sites. Readers are leaping to defend the restaurant, the food, and the chef. They even applaud the color of the dining area walls."

Aren grimaced. That comment came as a result of a line he'd written about the calming effect of the interior. The owners had chosen a warm shade of gray with black highlights. Aren might have gone a bit overboard when he'd insinuated that the interior, while soothing and inviting, wasn't enough to distract from the poor quality of the food. The remark had been cutting; he wished now he'd been more judicious.

"Not everyone is going to agree with me," he felt obliged to remind his editor.

"I second that. We aren't running a popularity contest with these restaurant reviews. However, when *three hundred* people take the time to write and contradict your findings, I sit up and take notice."

"Three hundred?" Aren squared his shoulders. "I ordered the sole—"

"I know what you ordered." She cut him off. "You wrote about it in great detail as part of your review."

She was right, he had.

"Look at this." Sandy swiveled her monitor around so Aren could read a few of the comments left on the website. In case he had trouble, Sandy read one aloud. "My name is Bill Wheeler and I've traveled extensively around the world. One of my favorite seafood dishes is sole served with a beurre blanc sauce. I've ordered sole in London, Paris, and beyond. The best, the very best I've ever tasted, is served at Heavenly Delights." The last three words were spoken slowly and precisely as though she was reading them to a child.

"Three hundred comments," Aren muttered under his breath.

"Apparently Mr. Wheeler liked it."

"Apparently so. Mine was inedible. An entire canister of salt must have fallen into that sauce, along with enough lemon to pickle herring, not to mention the distinct taste of cayenne pepper. There was no redeeming this sauce or the fish."

"Some people aren't going to agree with a food critic's reviews."

"That's understood."

"But three hundred? That tells me you aren't doing your job."

"That's not true." Aren feared he was about to join the ranks of the unemployed. "What would you like me to do?" he asked, fearing she was about to ask for his resignation.

"What I'd like," Sandy said, her voice elevated to the point that the window of her office vibrated, "is for you to eat at Heavenly Delights again. Clearly the chef had an off night."

"Clearly." Aren struggled to keep the sarcasm out of his voice.

"If several hundred diners have rallied to defend the chef, then I believe a second look is in order."

"All right." Although Aren wasn't looking forward to this dining experience.

"Do it soon."

"Consider it done. However . . ."

"Yes?" Sandy had already returned her attention to the computer screen. Her gaze bounced back to Aren.

"I wrote an honest review. I'm willing to give Heavenly Delights a second chance, but if the food is the same poor quality as before I won't change my opinion no matter how many people disagree with me."

"Fair enough," Sandy said. Then, as if she'd suddenly had a second thought, she asked, "Anyone go with you when you ate there earlier?"

"My sister."

"What was her opinion?"

Aren exhaled and frowned. "Actually, she was impressed. Her chicken dish was delicious, or so she claimed."

"So it was you and you alone who found the food below par."

"Apparently."

Sandy was facing her keyboard again even before he left the office. Returning to his desk, Aren reached for his cell and texted out a message to his sister.

Giving Heavenly Delights a second chance. Join me?

Her reply came within a few seconds. When?

Tonight?

Tomorrow?

OK tomorrow.

Can I meet you there?

No problem.

What time?

7 unless you hear otherwise.

Aren made the call and discovered, somewhat to his chagrin, that the only reservation available was for five thirty p.m. He sent another text to his sister.

She replied, I'll do my best to get there on time. Might be a few minutes late.

No problem.

Aren arrived at Heavenly Delights five minutes before their early reservation. His sister sent him a text telling him she was running ten minutes behind and told him to be seated.

Be there lickety-split.

The same charming, older woman who'd served as hostess at his first visit seated him. "I see you're back." She beamed him a smile. Then, lowering her voice, she added, "I'm glad that nasty food critic didn't change your mind about our food."

Aren feigned a grin.

She led him to a table that was close to the kitchen. He had to agree the scents coming from the other room enticed him.

Perhaps he had been overly critical. Well, he'd find out soon enough.

Chapter Seven

Busy in Heavenly Delights' kitchen, Lucie paused, certain she'd heard the sound of tinkling bells. The piped-in music was low and subtle but the gentle ring could be heard above and beyond that. Bells? Someone was ringing bells in the restaurant, and while that seemed rather odd, the melody resembled a favorite Christmas carol. "Jingle Bells."

Glancing outside the kitchen, thinking she might find the source, Lucie caught sight of someone who resembled . . . Aren.

It took a moment for her brain to register the fact that the man sitting at the table, reading over the menu, was indeed Aren Fairchild. Instantly her heart started racing at double time. Aren was here . . . in her restaurant? She swallowed hard, debating what to do . . . if anything. It'd been almost a year. She would hardly know what to say to him. How could she explain what had happened?

Mark, their headwaiter, stepped into the kitchen and Lucie grabbed him by the arm. "Get my mother."

Mark stared at her and his eyes rounded. "Now? Is everything all right?"

"Yes, I think so . . . just get my mother." She clenched her hands together and was grateful there was a lull in the kitchen. It was early—they had just opened for dinner—but soon the orders would come pouring in.

"Are you sure everything is all right?" Mark frowned, concerned.

Lucie had already started to shake. "Yes . . . of course."

Not more than a minute later Wendy raced into the kitchen. "Lucie, what's wrong?" She reached for Lucie's trembling hand.

"He's here . . . in the restaurant." But her mother seemed oblivious to whom she meant.

"Who's here, sweetheart?"

"Aren. Empire State Building Aren."

"Aren," her mother repeated slowly and then her eyes widened into round orbs. "That Aren?"

Biting into her lower lip, Lucie nodded. "And he's alone."

"That does it. You're coming with me."

"Mom . . ."

It was too late, her mother caught her by the sleeve of her cook's jacket and dragged Lucie through the swinging doors of the kitchen. Lucie knew the instant Aren saw her because his reaction was close to her own. The warm bread roll he held in his hand fell onto his plate and he slowly rose to his feet.

"Lucie?" Her name was a wisp of sound, as though he couldn't believe what he saw.

"Hello, Aren." Beyond a greeting she couldn't think of a single thing to say. Her tongue felt as if it'd grown to twice its normal size, filling her entire mouth and making speech impossible.

"I'm Lucie's mother, Wendy Ferrara." Her mother stepped forward and clasped Aren's hand with both of her own as if she were meeting a Greek god. She gazed up at him as though transfixed, studying his features as if wanting to memorize them.

Aren's gaze didn't waver from Lucie. Apparently he'd been struck with the same malady, because he didn't seem inclined to speak either.

"Did you . . . were you there?" Lucie didn't need to explain where she meant. Aren knew.

He broke eye contact and looked away before nodding.

Lucie felt dreadful to have left him to stand in the cold, believing she had chosen not to see him again. She would have given anything to live out her own version of *Sleepless in Seattle,* but apparently it wasn't meant to be. "Did you wait long?"

"Awhile." He shrugged as though it was nothing. "I left as soon as I realized you weren't coming."

Lucie noted that he didn't mention the length of time he'd stood in the cold and wind. She remembered that it had rained that day and hated the thought of him outside, dealing with the elements.

She hoped he'd been out of the cold. Lucie wanted to ask, but didn't.

"I'm so sorry," she whispered, and she was. Still, against impossible odds, they'd found each other again and now they couldn't seem to take their eyes off each other.

"Give him your phone number," her mother urged, poking Lucie in the side with her elbow. "Never mind, I'll do it, and listen, dinner is on us. Order anything you want."

Aren broke eye contact. "I can't let you do that."

"Please," Lucie added. "It's the least I can do."

Just then a lovely woman strolled up to the table. "It looks like we're having a party. Sorry I'm late."

Lucie's heart sank. She'd assumed Aren was dining alone. How foolish of her. How completely naive she was to entertain the idea that he'd pined for her the way she had for him. Clearly he'd met someone else. While Lucie was dressed in her kitchen gear with her hair tied up in a net, the other woman was striking in every sense of the word.

"Oh." Lucie retreated a step before Aren spoke.

"Lucie, this is my sister, Josie."

His sister? Lucie remembered that Aren had talked about his sister. He'd been living with her at the time.

"Lucie?" Josie asked, focusing her attention on her. "That Lucie?"

"Yes."

She noticed that he didn't elaborate beyond the one word. Apparently his sister knew all about her.

Ever the promoter, Wendy handed Aren a business card. "I've written Lucie's cell number on the back here. And, young man, you should know something . . ."

"Mom . . ." Lucie placed a restraining hand on her mother's arm.

Aren accepted the card and set it down on the tabletop.

Lucie hesitated. She really should get back to the kitchen. "Enjoy your dinner," she said in parting, retreating backward, one small step at a time. She bit her tongue to keep from telling him that she really would like to hear from him. The decision to contact her belonged to Aren. Now she would be the one left waiting and wondering.

Aren addressed her mother and sounded quite adamant. "Listen, I appreciate the offer but I insist upon paying for our meal."

"We'll argue about it later."

Although she was already in the kitchen, Lucie was able to overhear the conversation.

"I insist, Wendy. I will pay for our meal or Josie and I will need to leave."

Lucie heard her mother reluctantly acquiesce. Almost right away dinner orders started to come in and soon Lucie was preoccupied with cooking and getting food onto the plates. Within a matter of minutes she was so busy that she managed to put the fact that Aren sat only a few feet away out of her mind.

When next Lucie had the opportunity to look out to the dining area, she saw that another couple sat at the table where Aren and his sister had dined earlier.

Aren was gone.

Wendy had made certain that Aren had Lucie's cell number and she was left to wonder and hope he'd phone. Lucie wasn't finished cleaning the kitchen until after eleven. Her mother joined her and brought them each a cup of decaffeinated coffee.

"I see what you mean," her mother said, raising the cup to her lips. "Your Aren is real easy on the eyes."

"He isn't my Aren," she countered and then quickly added, "You think so?"

A smile quivered that her mother made no attempt to hide. "I wish you could have seen the look that came over you when you heard him say he'd been waiting for you."

"All these months. Oh, Mom, I feel dreadful."

"You wanted to meet him. Why wouldn't you let me tell him what happened and that you were on your way to meet him when the hospital phoned?"

Lucie wasn't sure. "The timing wasn't right. I figured it simply wasn't meant to be."

"What do you think now?"

Lucie was afraid to reveal how happy she was

that she'd found Aren. Although she'd worked a grueling shift, she wasn't tired. In fact, she was fairly certain she would have a hard time falling asleep. Her mind and her heart were filled with the hope of reconnecting with the man who'd swept her off her feet last New Year's Eve.

"Do you think he'll phone?" she asked her mother.

Wendy lowered her gaze to her coffee. "Sad to say, no."

Her heart plummeted. "He won't?"

"He said as much."

"You spoke to him after I went back to the kitchen?" Lucie had been too busy to pay attention to what had gone on after their initial meeting.

"At length."

"Mom!" It was just like Wendy to keep her in suspense like this.

"Sometimes I wonder about you, daughter."

"Why, what did I do now?"

Wendy shook her head. "Well, first off, you asked him how long he'd waited for you."

"Yes, I wondered . . . I mean, it's only natural to wonder if he had." He couldn't fault her for that.

"But you didn't bother to mention that you'd been on your way to meet him when you got the call from the hospital."

"I know . . ." Perhaps it'd been a mistake to keep silent.

Her mother sadly shook her head. "In fact, you didn't say a single word to encourage him."

Lucie's heart sank. Her mother was right.

Lucie was horrified at her thoughtlessness. "I noticed that he didn't really answer how long he'd waited for me."

"As well he shouldn't. Just think about it, Lucie. You stood him up and then asked him to confirm the fact."

Hearing it put like that made her feel sick to her stomach.

"Don't you think that was hard enough on his ego without you rubbing salt in his wound?"

Her mother was right. Lucie had messed up her chance with Aren royally. Not once, but twice. No wonder he'd made it clear he had no intention of contacting her. How completely dense she'd been. Hearing it now, and realizing how utterly foolish she'd been, made her want to weep.

Pushing the coffee aside, Lucie felt heartsick. "So he told you he has no intention of contacting me . . . ever."

"A man has his pride, Lucie."

"And I managed to stomp all over his."

"That you did," her mother said, and then hesitated. "However, Aren and I did manage to have a lengthy conversation."

Lucie's head snapped up. "What did he say?"

"Well, the truth of the matter is, I did most of the talking."

Oh, brother, this might not be good. "Mom,

what did you tell him?" Lucie waited, holding her breath.

"Lucie Ann, don't use that tone of voice with me. I simply explained that you had every intention of meeting him January 7, until you got the call from the hospital. I'm the one who caused you to miss that meeting. I assured Aren that I am not a busybody, but seeing that you failed to make your rendezvous because of me, I considered it my duty to set matters straight."

"What did he say to that?" Lucie leaned so close to her mother that she was in danger of falling off her stool.

"Well, right away I could see that Aren was grateful to learn the truth. He perked right up and so did his sister."

"He did?" Lucie frowned. "But you said he had no intention of calling me even though you gave him my cell number."

Her mother shook her head. "Give the man his due, daughter. His pride took a licking. He left his cellphone number with me and said if you were still interested then you should give him a call. You will, won't you?"

Lucie needed no time to make that decision. "I'll contact him first thing in the morning."

"Perfect."

Hungry for information, Lucie dug deeper. "Did you and Aren talk about anything else?"

Her mother hesitated. "Well, yes, and I hope I

didn't speak out of turn. I told him that you constantly scoured the newspaper looking for his byline."

"Oh, Mom." Lucie wished she hadn't.

"I could tell he was pleased to hear it."

"He was?" In retrospect, Aren deserved to know that Lucie hadn't forgotten him. Not a day passed that he didn't drift into her mind at one time or another. They'd been together only a few hours; nevertheless, Aren Fairchild had left a powerful impression on her.

"You ready to head home?" her mother asked.

Lucie nodded. "I bet you're tired."

"I'm fine. I've always enjoyed meeting people, but I do have to say, these dogs are barking." Removing her shoe, Wendy rubbed her sore toes.

"We did it," Mercy said and gave Goodness a high five.

"Aren didn't once wonder why Wendy seated him so close to the kitchen."

"That was an excellent idea even if I say so myself." Shirley's chest seemed to swell double in size.

Will looked unconvinced. "Would Gabriel call this Earthly interference?"

"No way," Shirley assured him. "It wasn't even close. If you want to talk about interference, then we can discuss the time Goodness took over that department store escalator or—"

"How did you get Lucie to look out of the kitchen when she did?" Will asked.

Mercy was grateful for the change of topic. She responded by pushing up the sleeves of her long white gown to reveal a row of small bells.

"The bells Lucie heard? That came from you?"

"That will be our little secret, okay?" Gabriel might not appreciate her sleight of hand . . . a small play on words there.

"Wow."

"It's a gift," Goodness explained, folding her hands and raising her head toward heaven with her eyes closed.

"You mean like peace, hope, mercy . . . that kind of godly gift."

"Ah, not exactly." They were leading Will down a slippery slope that made Mercy uncomfortable. "Actually, the bells are a small trick I learned years ago that I use on rare occasions."

"To garner humans' attention," Shirley supplied. "I remember once when Goodness appeared in church."

"She appeared in . . . bodily form as an angel?" This was one of the first lessons angels learned. Only those on direct assignment from God were allowed to appear as they were without disguise or dressed as ordinary humans. In all other instances they were to remain invisible or to take on human form.

"It was an emergency situation," Goodness clarified.

"It was necessary," Mercy seconded, "or Goodness would never have taken the risk."

Will looked to Goodness for an explanation.

"I appeared before a pastor who'd lost his wife to cancer."

"And with his wife he'd lost his faith, too," Shirley added.

Goodness's eyes brightened. "I wanted this poor grieving man to see God's love. I stood in the front of the church and in the full glory of God's grace I spread my wings and let my light shine."

Will's eyes grew huge and round. "What happened?"

Mercy came to stand closer to her friend. "Maybe we should see what Aren Fairchild is doing now that he's seen Lucie."

"No, wait," Will insisted, "tell me what happened to Goodness and the pastor. You have to tell me."

Goodness sighed and her shoulders and wings sank several inches. "He didn't see me."

"Didn't see you?" Will was incredulous. "How could he not see you? The light of God's love should have blinded him."

"He was too caught up in his grief."

"Oh dear," Will whispered, astonished.

"That's when I came up with the idea of the bells," Mercy explained. "It's a more subtle approach. The more time you spend dealing with humans the more you'll learn that one must be subtle."

"Most of the time delicate handling works," Shirley added.

"Most of the time," Mercy agreed, but then added under her breath, "but not all."

"Okay, let's find out what Aren's doing," Will said.

Chapter Eight

"You aren't going to call Lucie?" Josie demanded, sipping coffee from the disposable cup as they headed toward the subway station the following morning. "You're going to make her call you?"

Aren knew Josie couldn't possibly understand the dilemma he was in; well, then again, maybe she did. He had his pride, which was something his sister should understand. After all, it was pride that kept her from contacting Jack, even though Aren strongly suspected his sister was still in love with her former fiancé. She had been stingy with information as to what exactly had gone wrong. Although he was fairly certain it had something to do with the wedding, a disagreement, probably something silly, that had quickly escalated. Apparently it had grown to the point that they were convinced, one or the other, that marriage wasn't such a good idea after all. Following that, it made sense to assume they decided continuing their relationship wouldn't work either. Nerves stretched to the limit over a wedding and now Josie was alone and unhappy. Well, Aren and his sister made a great team, supporting each other in their misery.

His own relationship with Lucie was complicated and getting more so by the minute. It'd all seemed so perfect, innocent even, back on New Year's Eve. Now, with him working for the *Gazette* and Lucie part owner of the restaurant he'd reviewed, the possibility of him developing this relationship became that much more difficult.

"She'll be a fool if she doesn't contact you."

Aren and his sister had always been close. Every morning they walked to the subway together. He'd found an apartment close to Josie's and they met for coffee, carrying it with them as they headed toward their respective jobs.

"Maybe she wouldn't be such a fool." Aren had spent a sleepless night mulling over the impossibility of his situation. For one thing, he'd had a complete change of heart when it came to Heavenly Delights. Three hundred patrons hadn't been wrong. Dinner was a *delight* and the desserts afterward had been *heavenly*. His opinion had made a complete turnaround from his previous visit. This time it had earned its name. He'd told the managing editor he intended to write another review, and he would. Furthermore, his change of heart had nothing to do with his feelings toward the chef.

"By the way, is there any chance you can get tickets for *Angels at Christmas*?" Josie asked.

Naturally his sister would ask about the hottest

musical on Broadway. Tickets had been sold out months in advance. And with Christmas approaching they were impossible to find. "Yeah, right."

"Well, you just might. The newspaper has connections, doesn't it? It's just a matter of knowing the right people."

Aren snickered. As a recent hiree, he had little chance of getting tickets. He'd let Josie dream away. Aren enjoyed his sister's company, but if he took anyone to see a musical it would be Lucie; that is, if she wanted to see him again.

Following his divorce Aren hadn't leaped back into the dating world and noticed that Josie hadn't either, although she was quick to egg him on. Deep down Aren supposed his sister needed to see him willing to risk his heart again before she felt comfortable doing so herself. Brother and sister made a terrific dysfunctional team.

"Let me know what you find out," Josie murmured as she headed down to her train. "And if you do manage to get those tickets, ask Lucie."

Aren frowned. "I thought you wanted to go?"

"I will someday. I was just thinking it was an invitation Lucie wouldn't be able to turn down. I've heard that *Angels at Christmas* is an incredible musical."

"Don't hold your breath, okay?" He hated giving his thoughts away, and Lucie had definitely been heavy on his mind.

She gave him a cheery wave and was off.

Aren went to another track to catch his train and then walked the few blocks to the newspaper building. He dropped his backpack off at his desk and headed directly to Sandy's office.

The managing editor sat at her computer and glanced up when he knocked against the door frame. Looking at him above the glasses perched on the end of her nose, Sandy lifted her hands from the keyboard and swiveled her chair around. "You had dinner at Heavenly Delights?"

He nodded, stuffing the tips of his fingers in his jean pockets.

"And?"

"It was terrific."

She arched her brows as though pleasantly surprised. "So you had a change of heart."

He admitted as much. "I can't account for what happened the first time around. My sister was with me and her meal seemed to be just fine. Mine was a disaster."

"But not this time?"

"No, the sole was fabulous in every way." And in ways he hadn't expected that had nothing to do with the menu items.

"Good. Write your piece and we'll publish it in this evening's edition. That should make those supporters of the restaurant happy." As she spoke, his editor turned back to face her computer screen.

"Sandy," Aren said, remaining standing in the doorway to her office.

She looked his way, frowning with impatience. "Now what?"

"I can't write the review."

"Why not?" she demanded shortly, clearly irritated with him.

"I met the chef and I know her."

"Did that influence your opinion?"

"No."

"Then write the review."

"I'd like nothing better. However . . ."

She removed her glasses and glared up at him. "What's your problem, Fairchild?"

"I want to date the chef," he blurted out.

Sandy frowned and turned back to her computer again. "So date her. She doesn't need to know you're Eaton Well."

Aren was stunned. Not knowing what to expect from his admission, his mind started to spin with happy anticipation.

"Are you still here?" Sandy blurted out.

"Thanks, Sandy, really, I mean it. This is great news." Aren's heart was lighter than it'd been in months.

On his way in to talk to Sandy, he'd wondered what she'd say about him wanting to date Lucie. Now it felt as if the weight of ten dump trucks had been lifted from his shoulders.

Sandy glanced his way again. "Why are you still here?"

"No . . . no reason . . . I'm on my way to my desk

to write the finest restaurant review you've ever
published."

"Then get to it," she muttered gruffly.

No sooner had he sat down at his computer than
his cellphone buzzed. Distracted, Aren looked at it,
didn't recognize the number, and let whoever was
on the other end of the line talk to his voice mail.
He was about halfway through his review, which
literally seemed to be writing itself, when Norm
Lockett stopped by his cubicle. Norm did the reviews for Broadway shows.

"Norm," Aren called out, stopping him. "Can I
ask a favor?"

"What do you need, kid?"

Aren stood. Norm was thirty years his senior
and well liked by everyone. "Is there a possibility
of getting tickets for *Angels at Christmas*?" It
wouldn't do any harm to ask.

Norm grinned and slapped him across the back.
"Let me see what I can do."

"Thanks, Norm, I appreciate it." Then, because
he thought it might help, Aren added, "I don't suppose you heard Doris Roberts is coming in to re-
place the lead in *Angels at Christmas*?"

"I did."

The story had hit a few days earlier. Betty White
had come down with a nasty cold and needed a
break.

"I could write a short piece about Doris taking
over the role," Aren offered.

"No need," Norm said and slapped him across the back a second time. "I'll see what I can do, but no promises."

"Thanks," Aren said. "That would be great."

He returned to his cubicle and was absorbed in his writing when Norm returned. "This is your lucky day."

"You got tickets?"

"Two for next Thursday night."

Aren didn't care what night it was. "Thanks. You're the best." Aren was so pleased to get the tickets that he hadn't even bothered to check his own schedule. Once he did, he discovered he had another restaurant review arranged for the same night. Dinner and a show. He could hardly believe his luck. Heaven was looking favorably down on him this fine December day. It would be even better if Lucie contacted him. If not, then he'd take his sister.

Norm returned to his cubicle and Aren went back to writing the review for Heavenly Delights. The words flowed effortlessly and he was humming right along when he paused mid-word. A thought struck him. The call he'd sent to voice mail earlier might have been Lucie.

Grabbing his cell, he played back the message. Sure enough, just as he'd suspected.

"Hello, Aren, this is Lucie. Mom said she explained why I didn't meet you last January. I'm sorry you were left waiting. I'm hoping that you'd

be willing to give me another chance. If you are, then give me a call, and if not . . . well, I understand." Her voice dipped with dread or disappointment, Aren didn't know which.

He couldn't push the button fast enough to call her back.

She answered with, "This is Lucie."

"Aren," he supplied, but before he could get another word out, Lucie started jabbering away.

"Oh, Aren, you got my call. Obviously you did, otherwise you wouldn't be phoning me. I sound completely redundant, don't I? It's just that I'm so very pleased to hear from you." She paused as if embarrassed at how fast she'd spoken. "I'll shut up and let you talk now."

Aren smiled and a warm happiness settled over him. "You can keep talking as long as you like. I like the sound of your voice."

"You do?"

"It's providential that we should meet after all these months, don't you think?" he asked.

"Yes . . . and providential is the perfect word, but then you work with words, don't you?"

"I do."

"Mom said you were writing for the paper. I'd looked for your name—"

"I'm not exactly their ace reporter."

"No, but you're a wonderful writer . . . at least I think you must be, even if I haven't read anything you've written."

Actually, she had read one of his most significant pieces—his review of her restaurant. But Aren couldn't tell her that, his contract at the paper stated as much and the managing editor had taken pains to remind him. Even if he was able, he wouldn't. He didn't want to end a promising relationship when it was just getting started.

Using this opportunity to change the subject he said, "I called because I was wondering if you'd be available for dinner and a show next week. I have two tickets to *Angels at Christmas* next Thursday."

"*Angels at Christmas*! I heard it was impossible to get tickets for that musical."

"I have two."

"But, oh dear, I . . . don't think I can. I'm cooking at the restaurant in the evenings."

Of course she was. Aren couldn't believe he'd forgotten that one key element. "Naturally you'd be working; I was so excited about the tickets I completely forgot."

"Thursday night you say?" The question was followed by a short hesitation. "Listen, it doesn't matter what night it is because I'm taking it off. We have a really wonderful sous-chef who can cover for me. I attended culinary school with Catherine— she's really good. My mother's been after me to take a break and this is important. Not to the world in general important, but important to me. Oh heaven, I'm doing it again. I probably don't make any sense whatsoever, do I?"

"Amazingly, you do." Aren's grin was so wide it hurt his face. "I'll see you next week then."

"Okay. Will you call me with the time or should I phone you?"

"I'll be in touch."

"Wonderful. Thank you for calling me back, Aren."

He should be the one thanking her. They said their farewells and Aren felt like he could climb a mountain. Returning to the task at hand, he waited a few minutes and then reached for his phone to contact his sister.

Josie answered almost immediately. She worked on Wall Street for a large brokerage firm.

"I have good news, good news, and bad news."

"Do tell."

"I heard from Lucie." He could have tried to play it cool, but his sister knew him far too well. She'd read through his blasé attitude in one second flat. Fooling Josie would be near impossible; consequently he didn't even try.

"She called already?"

"A few minutes ago."

"You're going to see her, aren't you?"

"Yup. That's the good news and the bad news."

"Explain yourself, little brother."

"I'm taking her to dinner and a show."

"Wow, you sure know how to sweep a girl off her feet. Which show?"

"That's the bad news."

A short hesitation followed. "Don't tell me . . . you have tickets to *Angels at Christmas*?"

"I do."

"Aww, man."

"Don't hate me," Aren teased. "I have other good news, too, but I didn't want to overwhelm you."

"You might as well kick me harder. I suppose they're orchestra seats." She laughed and Aren knew she was happy that Lucie had agreed to go with him.

"As far as I'm concerned they could be in the nosebleed section and I wouldn't care. My third bit of good news is that I talked to my boss and Sandy said it would be fine for me to write the review for Heavenly Delights, and retract my previous one."

"Well, duh, of course you should."

"I feared it might be considered a conflict of interest, but Sandy basically said not to worry about it as long as I don't reveal my identity."

"Good . . . but does Lucie or her mother know you're the one who wrote the initial review, panning the restaurant?"

"No."

"No? Aren, this could come back to bite you."

"I'll tell her when the time is right. I don't want to hide it from her but my contract states that I can't let anyone know my identity outside of family. Besides, Lucie and I just reconnected."

"And you don't want to upset the proverbial apple cart."

"Something like that," he admitted. In his mind he had the perfect excuse.

"Oh, Aren, promise me you won't keep it a secret for long."

"Josie, I'm under contract. I could lose my job if I tell her I'm writing as Eaton Well."

"There are ways you can do it without saying it directly, you know."

"Maybe," he countered. "But it's too soon."

"Okay, I agree with you there, but I'm afraid this is going to hang over your head like a giant water balloon, threatening to burst at any moment."

"I'll find the right time," he promised. "But not until I can figure out a way to do it without actually telling her and until we've had a chance to get to know each other better. Agreed?"

"Okay, but don't wait until it's too late."

"I won't." This would be tricky, but he'd look for a way, and for a time when it was right.

Chapter Nine

"Get a load of those angels on stage," Mercy muttered, shaking her head in exasperation. "Apparently this is humanity's idea of what we look like. Oh dear, these poor people don't have a clue."

Shirley, Goodness, and Mercy, along with Will, sat in the box seat section of the Broadway theater and found themselves highly amused by the musical. After strict instructions from Gabriel they knew better than to interfere with the budding romance between Lucie and Aren. This was a hands-off assignment.

Still, Mercy kept a close eye on the two. They had great seats about ten rows back in the orchestra section and seemed to be enjoying the musical immensely. Every now and again their heads would come together and they'd exchange whispers. Mercy had a bit of a romantic streak and it seemed the couple was perfect together. Her heart swelled with appreciation when shortly after the musical started Aren reached for Lucie's hand and she smiled ever so sweetly up at him. It was the most romantic moment Mercy had seen in a very long while.

When Mercy's gaze wandered back to her friends, she froze as an odd sensation went through her.

Goodness had disappeared.

"Where's Goodness?" she whispered, fighting down dread.

Shirley shrugged, apparently caught up in what was happening on stage.

"Will, have you seen Goodness?" she asked, hoping to hide the panic in her voice.

Their young charge seemed to find the antics on stage highly amusing, and he answered with a shake of his head.

Mercy frantically glanced around and soon saw that her worst fears were about to take place. Goodness was on stage with the actors. Not knowing what else to do, and intent on avoiding another disaster, Mercy quickly joined her friend, grabbing Goodness by the arm. "What are you doing here?" she whispered.

"These actors don't know anything about angels or how we behave. Their costumes are a joke."

Oh dear, it was worse than she thought. "Goodness, don't even think about it."

"I just want to ruffle their feathers a little, make them a bit more presentable. Gabriel would want that."

"No, he wouldn't," Shirley chimed in. The three

of them bounced around the stage, flittering from one part to another, avoiding the actors.

"What's that?" Will asked, joining them.

"What's what?"

"That man. He's playing some sort of musical instrument."

"It's a tuba, now go back where we were," Mercy instructed.

All at once one of the stage angels let out a screech as she was suspended two feet off the ground. "Goodness, mercy," the actor cried, frantically flapping her arms.

"She knows our names," Shirley said, aghast.

"Put her down," Mercy pleaded, and quickly amended. "Gently, please."

The actor's feet gradually returned to the stage and almost immediately three other stage angels were elevated. Not knowing what was happening, the other actors, obviously skilled professionals, continued with their lines as if nothing were amiss, craning their necks in order to look up at the actors whose feet were scrambling and arms flapping. Apparently the audience took it all in their stride, laughing uproariously. Those viewing the show seemed to believe this was part and parcel of the program, which was a play within a play.

The main characters had attended a Christmas program in which the children reenacted the Nativity scene. The angels, all actors, played major roles, directing the children. Now Shirley, Goodness, and Mercy caused near pandemonium with the stage crew shrugging their shoulders, running onto the stage, and looking up for some nonexistent hidden wire.

While Mercy argued with Goodness, sensible Shirley had apparently lost her head and decided this was her moment to shine. Mercy couldn't believe her eyes when her fellow Prayer Ambassador broke into song along with the small children's choir.

Seeing that it was a lost cause, Mercy gave up and joined her friend, singing one of their favorite Christmas carols. Everyone on stage froze and stared at the children and for one short moment, Mercy feared they were about to be discovered.

"I think it's time we go now," Will said, tugging at Shirley's sleeve.

"Oh dear, you might be right," Shirley said, seemingly coming to her senses.

"I'd like to try playing that tuba before we go," Will said, heading for the orchestra pit.

Goodness grabbed Will and hauled him back.

"Not now," Mercy pleaded, ushering the other three off the stage. "We need to get while the getting is good."

Oh dear, this was going badly.

"What about Lucie and Aren?" Will protested as they made their way back to heaven. "Can we just leave them behind?"

"We don't have any choice now." Mercy wasn't sure how everything had gotten out of hand like this, but it was beyond redemption now. Oh, she should have known, should have guessed, that seeing angels on stage would be too much temptation for them. They left the theater and Mercy had started to relax when she heard Shirley screech. "Goodness! Put the camel back before anyone notices it's missing."

Mercy looked back and gasped. Sure enough her dear friend had stolen the camel that was tethered backstage and was leading him down the street.

Yup, they were beyond redemption. All Mercy could hope was that heaven didn't hear about this until much, much later.

"What did you think of the musical?" Aren asked Lucie as they slowly made their way out of the theater.

It was difficult for her to hear him above the excited chatter of the crowd. Everyone was talking about the performance. Lucie overheard someone say that they'd seen the same play earlier and that she really liked the additional comedic changes.

"I thought it was amazing . . . simply amazing."

"I did, too," Aren agreed.

Once outside, he helped Lucie on with her coat and then buttoned his own. He reached for her hand and tucked it in the crook of his elbow. It was a cold night, which gave Lucie a good excuse to stay close to Aren. The lights in the city over the holidays seemed to glow a little brighter. Everything felt so perfect, so wonderful. Although she'd known Aren only a short while, it seemed that he'd always been in her life. Never having experienced that kind of connection with a man before, Lucie couldn't help but wonder if she'd found the man she could love with the same intensity as the love her parents had shared.

"I'm still trying to figure out how they managed to elevate the angels," Aren remarked, frowning as he spoke. "Usually I can see the wires, and we were close enough to get a good look, but I didn't see any."

"The children's singing was . . . unbelievable."

"I'm going to download the music as soon as I get home. It was . . ." Aren seemed to be searching for the right word.

"Angelic," Lucie supplied. Their shoulders touched as they walked, arm in arm. "I had the most wonderful evening. I don't know how to thank you."

Aren grinned and wrapped his hand around hers in the crook of his elbow. "We're not finished yet."

"We're not?"

"I hope you're hungry."

"Starved." Lucie had gotten up extra early that morning to bake and get everything ready at the restaurant so she could leave for the night in good conscience. It'd been tempting to phone in and make sure everything was going okay. But her mother had discouraged that. Wendy wanted Lucie to forget about the restaurant for one night and enjoy herself. Lucie didn't think it was possible, but she was wrong. When she was with Aren it felt as if she didn't have a care in the world.

"I know it's late but I made dinner reservations."

They walked past Rockefeller Center and paused to admire the lights on the Christmas tree and gaze at the skaters circling the ice. Unable to resist, Lucie pressed her head against Aren's shoulder.

"Tired?"

She should be, but she wasn't. "No, just happy, so happy."

"I am, too. I didn't think it was possible to find you again."

"I didn't either. I'd given up hope."

They continued walking, their pace slow and easy until they arrived at the restaurant, which carried the name of a well-known television chef. Lucie couldn't help being impressed.

"How did you manage this along with the theater tickets to the hottest show in town?"

He grinned sheepishly. "I pulled a few strings."

"I've heard so much about the food here. I've always wanted to try it."

"Good, this is my first experience, too."

Now she understood why he'd chosen to eat so late. This was probably the only time he could get a reservation. From everything Lucie had heard, the restaurant was booked months in advance. It was next to impossible to get in during the holidays. Lucie could only speculate as to how many favors Aren would owe for this night. Certainly she would long remember this evening.

After they were seated they waited several minutes before the menus were delivered. Lucie caught Aren's eye. "Mom would never let that happen," she whispered.

"Oh?"

"Waiting for the menus. She'd be on that right away."

Aren grinned and opened the elaborately framed menu. A gold tassel dangled at the bottom.

After giving them more than ample time to study the meal selections the waiter returned and recited the evening's specials in elaborate detail, mentioning the country of origin for the herbs and spices and every nuance of each particular dish. Because it was late in the evening they'd sold out of the appetizer and had only one of the special entrées left.

Again Lucie had trouble hiding a frown. "Why mention the specials at all if they aren't available? All those details didn't make the dish sound more appealing. He made me feel it should be placed in a museum to be admired."

"I agree," Aren said, chuckling softly.

Lucie ordered the Chilean sea bass and Aren asked for cheese-stuffed chilies. Once served, the food was as much a disappointment as the service had been.

"Well, what do you think?" Aren asked after

she'd taken her first bite. "Does this restaurant live up to its reputation?"

Lucie set her fork aside and weighed whether she should speak her mind or not. Being in the restaurant business herself, she suspected she was being overly critical. Aren had gone to a lot of trouble to get this reservation, but she could see he wasn't enjoying his dinner either. "Do you want the truth?" she asked.

"Of course."

"The fact is I'm disappointed, but take that with a grain of salt. I know a lot about running a restaurant. My fish was overcooked, the sauce has no flavor, and the vegetables have had the very life boiled out of them. This is what drives me crazy."

"Oh?"

"We had a food critic visit our restaurant who lambasted my cooking. He or she was cruel and mean and I'm telling you right now, I'll put every dish I serve up against this restaurant's any day of the week."

Aren stared across the table at her with his fork frozen in midair.

Lucie should have taken that as a sign to stop talking, but once she got started she couldn't seem to stop. "What upsets me is that this very same food critic would probably give this restaurant high marks. I mean, Eaton Well must have reviewed the meals here for it to have such a fabulous reputation. That just goes to show you the critic doesn't know what he's talking about." She bit down on her lip, recognizing that she'd probably said far too much. Every time she thought about Eaton Well and his unfair and cutting review, Lucie's blood boiled. Because she felt she had to, Lucie added, "I know he works for the same newspaper as you, and if he's a friend then I apologize. It's just that he did me wrong and I don't know that I could ever forgive what he said about Heavenly Delights."

Aren continued to stare at her as if he didn't know what to say. Lucie tried again, fearing she'd ruined their evening with her tirade. "Forgive me, please," she murmured, smoothing out the linen napkin in her lap. "I shouldn't have mentioned the review. As you might have guessed I'm still upset about it."

Aren reached for his coffee, which had grown cold by now. "From what your mother said, your loyal customers were quick to come to your defense."

"Yes, thank heaven. Without them we might have been ruined. We could have lost everything because of one negative review."

Aren returned the cup to the saucer and leaned back, but she could see that he wasn't relaxed. "There was a second review, wasn't there?"

"Yes, a retraction. Apparently good ol' Eaton Well was forced into giving the restaurant a second chance."

"Was his second review fair?"

"I suppose," she said with a shrug. "Still, I'd like

to meet the man just so I could give that jerk a piece of my mind."

"Jerk?"

"Well, in my mind he is. Why is it people have to be so cutting and heartless? The things he said were completely unnecessary. Do these writers honestly think they're being witty? Don't they realize people's livelihoods are at stake?"

"I'm sure everything will work out in the end."

"I hope so."

To her surprise Aren ordered a dessert tray with small selections of a number of desserts. Lucie sampled a taste of a couple of the ones she thought sounded appealing—the banana cream cake and the raspberry sorbet. Both were adequate but nothing to rave about.

"Your desserts taste far better."

She beamed with his praise and silently agreed with him. As it was she'd already said far too much about the food and the service. "Thank you."

Aren paid the bill, which to Lucie's way of thinking was outlandish for what they'd received. As they left the restaurant, he seemed more subdued than earlier. Perhaps, like her, his day had been long and he was tired. It was late and they both had to work in the morning.

"Tell you what," she said as they strolled down the street. "Let me cook you a real dinner. This one was a disappointment and I'd like to treat you to one of my meals created especially for you."

Aren glanced over at her and smiled. "I'm not turning this down."

"Good. Would Sunday afternoon work for you?" Already her mind buzzed with ideas. Cooking was an emotional experience and Lucie found it easier to express her feelings through food than with words. Dinner would be her way of letting Aren know how much she enjoyed his company and how very grateful she was that they'd reconnected.

"Sunday will work out just fine."

"Great. Come to my apartment about four . . . if that's not too early."

"It's perfect."

Aren stopped walking and signaled for a taxi.

"I had the most wonderful evening," she said, knowing their time was about to come to an end. "Thank you, Aren, for everything."

A cab pulled up to the curb. Aren opened the passenger door and Lucie instinctively rose on her tiptoes to kiss him. She'd waited a long time for this, wondering if the kiss she remembered on New Year's nearly a year ago would measure up.

Aren gripped her by the shoulders and slanted his mouth over hers.

Oh, it was good, as good as she remembered, perhaps even better. She wanted to melt into his arms, and resisted the urge to wrap herself all around him, feet and hands, arms and legs.

"Hey, you two," the cabbie called out, "I don't have all night."

Lucie tasted Aren's reluctance as he gradually released her. "We'll talk before Sunday, okay?"

"Of course."

He looked so serious, even deeply troubled, but Lucie couldn't imagine what it might be. The evening had been nearly perfect . . . other than the dinner, but that wasn't Aren's fault.

Once she was inside the cab, Aren stepped back and lifted his hand in farewell.

Pressing her fingers to her lips, she set her hand against the window as the cabbie drove off.

Chapter Ten

Aren stood patiently in line at the Starbucks, dreading having to face his sister. He didn't need to wait long before Josie sashayed into the coffeehouse no more than five minutes after he arrived.

He purchased both their coffees.

"Hey, to what do I owe this?" she asked when he handed her the disposable cup.

Aren didn't have an answer. He knew she was waiting to hear about his evening with Lucie, and it had been wonderful, better than he'd hoped. What troubled him was how angry Lucie was at Eaton Well and that original review. She hardly took into account the second review in which he'd praised her and highly recommended Heavenly Delights. It was almost as if the favorable review hadn't counted.

They started walking toward the subway, their steps perfectly in tune with each other's. "Well, don't keep me in suspense," she said, "tell me how it went with Lucie last night."

"Great."

"You don't sound like it was great. Oh, Aren, don't tell me, did she guess who you are?" Josie abruptly stopped, causing the people behind her to come to a halt and forcing them to walk around Josie and Aren, muttering as they passed by.

Aren was forced to stop, too. "No, but she talked plenty about the *jerk* who nearly destroyed their reputation with a bad review."

"You didn't tell her it was you, did you?" Josie demanded.

"I couldn't." He didn't know how many times he needed to remind his sister he was under contract.

Josie tilted back her head and looked at the darkening sky as though the frustration was too much for her. "Oh, Aren, this isn't good."

He'd thought about nothing else all night. Lucie needed to know, and the longer he kept it a secret, the more difficult it would become for him once the truth came out.

They started walking again, fast approaching the subway station.

"What did Lucie say?" Josie pressed.

Aren shrugged as if he didn't remember, although he did, almost every word. "She talked about Eaton Well and how mean and unfair he was. At one point she even said she'd like to meet him just so she could tell him off."

"Oh boy."

"Even if I could tell her I wouldn't . . . not with everything going so well. She's still so angry."

"But you wrote a wonderful review later."

"I mentioned that, but she brushed it off, discounting the article. She couldn't talk about anything but the first review."

"But Aren, you've got to find a way to let her know sooner or later."

Aren didn't need his sister to tell him that. He knew. "I agree."

"You of all people know what it's like to be deceived. I know it's a risk, but it's one you have to take."

In theory Aren couldn't fault her logic. "I know what needs to be done, it's just that . . . I don't know how to do it and not break my agreement with the newspaper. Have you ever met someone you instantly clicked with? Lucie is smart and funny and intensely loyal and kind. She loves her family and her dog and you should see the way everyone at the restaurant feels about her and her mother. I don't know when I've ever met a better group of people."

"You've only been there twice."

"I know, and it isn't what they say, it's how they all work together and support one another. That kind of camaraderie starts with management and works its way down. Lucie and her mother are destined to make Heavenly Delights a success. I can already see it."

"All I can say is that you need to find a way to tell

Lucie before this whole situation blows up in your face."

Aren couldn't put up a single argument. "She invited me to dinner at her apartment on Sunday."

Josie took a swig of coffee and shook her head. "You've got to find a way before then."

"But . . ."

"It'll only get harder, the longer you put it off."

Aren's breath came out in foggy bursts in the cold. Snow had started to fall and while the signs of Christmas were all around him, he barely noticed.

"I'll think of something," he murmured, and he would.

Josie was right. He stood to lose both his job and Lucie, but it was a risk he had to take. "I'll think of something." It wouldn't be easy but it simply had to be done.

"Call me when you come up with an idea."

He promised he would even as the dread settled over him.

"Okay, now that that's over with," Josie continued as if she were glad to set aside the subject. "Tell me what happened at the play last night."

Aren smiled at the memory. "*Angels at Christmas* was great, better than expected."

"It's been all over the news this morning, didn't you hear?"

"Hear what?"

"Aren, good grief, you were there! You must have seen it."

He felt totally perplexed; he didn't have a clue what his sister was talking about.

"The actors were interviewed and they told this unbelievable story about how they were lifted two and three feet off the ground. They were reciting their lines the way they do every performance, and all of a sudden they were lifted off their feet and suspended in the air for several minutes."

Of course Aren remembered. Lucie and he had talked about not being able to see the wires. "You mean that wasn't part of the play?"

"No, and then another group of performers insisted someone else was singing with them. Actually more than one person."

"The music was out of this world," Aren agreed.

"Critics are saying it's a publicity stunt and the actors insist it wasn't. Everyone is talking about it on the radio this morning. And you know, I tend to agree with those critics. It sounds like some sort of publicity prank. I mean, how else do you explain that camel wandering down Broadway with trainers chasing after it?"

"The camel got loose?" Aren hadn't heard a word about any of this.

"Honestly, Aren, you've got to get your head out of the clouds. This thing with Lucie is muddling up your brain."

His brain was more than messed up. All he could

think about was Lucie and how afraid he was of losing her again so soon after they'd found each other. That morning he'd turned on the radio but his thoughts had been wrapped around Lucie, and apparently he hadn't been listening.

They parted soon afterward. Josie went in one direction and he took off in another.

Aren spent the better part of the day writing the review on his experience at the restaurant. Then, because he'd been at the play the night before, he was asked to write a short piece about what he saw and his own interpretation of the strange events from the night before, which was scheduled to run in that evening's issue. The restaurant review took more time. He deliberately placed Lucie's comments from the dinner as part of the piece. Once she read the article written by Eaton Well she'd know who he was and then they could talk freely. If she hated him, well, it would be a clean break before his heart was even more heavily involved. When he handed in his article, the feedback was positive.

From the office he caught the subway to Brooklyn. The sky was dark; snow had fallen intermittently all day so that a soft layer of white covered the landscape. Schoolchildren were out and about and Aren counted several snowmen as he walked to Heavenly Delights. Under normal circumstances he would have taken a cab, but he wanted to clear his head.

The restaurant had been open only a few minutes

when he arrived. Wendy Ferrara's face broke into a brilliant smile the instant Aren stepped into the restaurant.

"Aren, how good to see you." She greeted him like family with a kiss on the cheek. "Lucie had such a wonderful time last evening; it was all she could talk about this morning."

"I had a great time myself."

"Here, sit down. I'll get you a hot cup of coffee. It's freezing out there and you're half frozen." She led the way to a table.

Before Aren could protest, Wendy was off to the kitchen.

Having no choice, Aren sat down and looked around. The restaurant had been decorated for the holidays since his last visit. Each table held a sprig of holly around the base of a thick round candle and was set with green and red linen napkins. A swag of silver tinsel surrounded the hostess desk and two glass ornaments dangled across the front with Wendy and Lucie's names printed on them. Another glittery swag was draped across the length of windows with identical ornaments with the employees' names written for all to read.

Wendy returned a moment later, carrying a steaming cup of coffee. Aren would gladly have gone without it, but she was right, he was cold.

"I hope you don't mind but Lucie had to step out for a quick errand. She should only be a few minutes. I apologize, she must have forgotten you were stopping by."

"She didn't know . . . it was a spur-of-the-moment decision."

"Ah, that explains it. She's quite taken with you, you know," Wendy told him.

Hearing that was like listening to those incredible singing voices at the play all over again. His sister was right. What happened at the show was all over the news. Once word got out that he'd attended, Aren lost count of the number of people who stopped by his cubicle to ask about it. He wished he'd paid more attention. At the time, the antics of the angels had all seemed so natural, as if it was intentional. People get elevated on stage all the time. Good grief, Spider-Man darted all over the audience from one side of the theater to the other and no one had made much of a fuss about that. But then the wires were clearly visible.

"I think the world of Lucie, too."

"Can I get you anything to eat?" Wendy asked.

"No thanks. I stopped by to have a quick word with Lucie and then I need to go."

"Then I'll pack up a dinner for you to take with you."

Aren raised his hand in protest. "Please, Mrs. Ferrara, that won't be necessary."

"Nonsense. I won't take no for an answer."

Before he could protest further, Wendy disappeared inside the kitchen. When she returned she brought out a large paper bag. If the size of the container was any indication, he'd have enough food for a week.

"I phoned Lucie and she's on her way. She asked me to keep you here no matter what."

Aren had no real reason for his visit other than the need to see Lucie again and the fear he was about to lose her.

"What's going to happen?" Will asked. He frowned with concern almost as if he knew in advance what was about to take place. "When Lucie learns Aren wrote the negative review, she's going to be terribly upset."

"I'd be upset, too," Shirley agreed. "There simply must be something we can do to help. I don't understand why Aren insists on ruining such a promising relationship."

"We can't interfere," Goodness insisted, regarding the others. "Gabriel wouldn't like it."

"He wouldn't like you absconding with a camel either, but that didn't stop you from pilfering it right off the stage," Mercy reminded her dearest friend.

Goodness had the good grace to look more than a little chagrined. "That was a momentary slip in judgment. Has . . . anyone heard from Gabriel yet?"

"No, and kindly lower your voice before he does hear."

Mercy did a rapid three-sixty, certain Gabriel would appear at any moment and banish them from Earth forever.

"I say we keep our shenanigans to ourselves for now."

"If we can," Goodness whispered, and glanced over her shoulder.

"What about Aren and Lucie?" Will persisted, sitting impatiently in a corner of the restaurant. "What's going to happen?" He flittered about the room, revealing his nervousness.

"We won't know until later when she reads the article," Mercy explained. She worried about the young couple as much as Will, but the future was held in God's hands.

The three of them plus Will hovered above the restaurant, waiting for Lucie to arrive. Mercy noticed that the tables filled up fast. When Lucie rushed into the kitchen, she was immediately inundated with meal orders.

"Is Aren going to talk to her?" Will asked.

"It looks like he wants to try," Mercy said, closely watching the scene as it unfolded with Aren in the kitchen with Lucie.

Aren followed Lucie all around the busy kitchen. He had trouble keeping up with her. He found it amazing she could accomplish as much as she did in such a compressed space, especially with two other workers darting this way and that.

"It's so good to see you," she said, swirling fresh sliced mushrooms around a pan over the gas-fired stove. She paused just long enough to smile over at him. "I loved every minute of our night. Thank you again for everything."

Dismissing her gratitude, he drew in a deep breath and said, "I know this isn't the best time." The words were barely out of his mouth when Lucie abruptly turned and opened the refrigerator. He jerked out of her way as she grabbed what she needed and returned to the stove. "I hoped we might have a few minutes to chat." He intended to mention the piece he wrote and ask her not to read it until they'd had a chance to be together.

"Oh, Aren, I'd like nothing better, but as you can see I've got my hands full at the moment."

Speaking of hands, Aren was forced to back into the sink and raise his arms above his head as Lucie flew past him. Clearly this wasn't working.

"Can't we talk Sunday?" she asked.

"Ah . . . sure." The review was scheduled to be printed in the Saturday edition.

"Great."

"I apologize for stopping off without calling first. . . . I should have realized. Sunday, then."

"Sunday," Lucie echoed. "Then I'll be able to give you my full attention."

"Okay." Aren's shoulders sagged with frustration and discouragement as he started out of the kitchen.

"Aren, hold up a minute," Lucie called out, stopping him.

Just before he walked away, Lucie came to him, placed her hands on his shoulders, and then gently pressed her lips to his. Aren felt that kiss all the way to the bottom of his feet, his nerve endings sizzling, and when she stepped back it was all he could do to remain standing.

"Will that hold you until Sunday?" she asked with a saucy grin.

Aren needed to clear his throat before he was able to speak. "It should."

"Good."

The kiss held him all the way back to Manhattan. By then his head had cleared and the buzz on his phone told him he had a text. Even without looking Aren knew it was from Josie.

Well? No doubt she'd been waiting all day to hear how he intended to handle this difficult situation.

I wrote my piece and used her quotes. She'll recognize who I am the minute she picks up the newspaper. He needed to wait only a few seconds for her reply.

That'll do it all right. Are you at peace with whatever happens?

Aren hated waiting; it made everything worse.

I think so.

Not two seconds after he sent his message, he received an answer back.

Fingers crossed.

He wanted to mention the article to Lucie, but it had been impossible to hold any kind of conversation while she was cooking. He'd done his best but it seemed as if the forces of nature were against him.

He texted back. Have dinner with me. Meet me in 15 and I'll explain. Lucie's mother gave me a to-go box.

Josie's response was fast in coming. This better be good.

Aren grinned and quickly typed: Dinner or my excuse?

Both.

Chapter Eleven

Saturday afternoon, Lucie reached for her cell and went to her contact list. She pushed Aren's name and number. After three rings, he answered. "Aren, here."

"What are you doing?" she asked.

"Lucie?"

He sounded both pleased and surprised to hear from her, which boosted her confidence. "Yup, it's me."

"What am I doing? Nothing much. I just finished my laundry and cleaning my apartment. I save everything for the weekend. We're still meeting tomorrow for dinner, aren't we?"

"I'm planning on it."

"What's up?"

"Would you like to work for your dinner?"

"Ah, sure. What do you have in mind?"

"Meet me in half an hour," she said and gave him the address.

"You aren't at the restaurant?"

"Not now, but I will be later. This is something special."

"Special. Do you want to give me a hint?"

"Nope. It's a surprise. You showed me such a wonderful time I thought I would return the favor."

"I thought dinner on Sunday was that."

"This is something . . . extra. Mom is with me so don't be late."

Aren chuckled. "I'm on my way."

Lucie ended the call.

"You got ahold of him?" Wendy asked, tying the apron around her middle. The meal was almost ready to serve. Two hundred fifty meals, to be exact. Roast beef, mashed potatoes with gravy, fresh green beans, a homemade roll still warm from the oven, and chocolate cake.

"Aren's on his way."

"Did you tell him this is a soup kitchen?"

Lucie did her best to hide a smile. "I might have forgotten to mention that." She returned to the Salvation Army kitchen and put the finishing touches on the gravy. Within a few minutes the doors would open and the homeless men and women would pour into the dining hall. After reaching for trays and plates, Wendy, Lucie, and Aren would serve the homeless as they went through the line. Wendy would dish up the meat and potatoes, Aren was assigned the vegetables and gravy, and Lucie planned to finish up with the roll and cake. Drinks were on the sideboard and the paid staff would see to keeping the coffee, tea, milk, and water replenished.

As long as Lucie could remember, she and her mother had volunteered at the shelter in December. She'd have just enough time to serve dinner here before heading out to cook at Heavenly Delights. Her day had been jam-packed from early morning, starting with the baking and menu planning. Her head was buzzing with everything she had to do when Jazmine phoned to say she'd come down with the flu. That meant Lucie and her mom would be short one person for serving dinner. Lucie had immediately thought of Aren.

"I'll finish up here," her mother told her. "If you didn't explain what this is all about, Aren will assume he has the wrong address."

"You think I should go outside and wait for him?"

"Yes, sweetie, otherwise he'll be confused."

Lucie knew her mother was right. Grabbing her coat, she stepped into the wind and cold of the late afternoon. The gloomy skies threatened more snow, which she didn't mind. Snowfall made the holiday season all the more festive.

As she paced the area she thought about the men and women without anyplace warm to sleep. Well, for tonight they would have a hot, nutritious meal to fill their stomachs.

A taxi pulled up across the street and Aren climbed out, frowning. He glanced down at a slip of paper in his hand. Her mother was right. He was confused.

"Aren," Lucie called, waving her arm above her head in order to get his attention, while clenching her coat closed at her neck. She marveled that he'd been so willing to come even without any details.

His face relaxed when he saw her and after looking both ways, he raced across the street.

"What is this?"

"A homeless shelter. Mom and I volunteer and we're short one person. Can you help?"

"I'd love to . . . only can we talk afterward?"

Her shoulders sagged with disappointment. "Oh, Aren, I can't. I'm so sorry. I have to leave as soon as we're finished to get to the restaurant."

He expelled his breath. "Did you read the paper this morning?"

"No," she admitted. There simply hadn't been time. But there could be only one reason he'd asked. "Did the paper print one of your articles? Did you get a byline? Finally! Oh, Aren, you must be so pleased. I'll get a newspaper as soon as I can."

He didn't answer right away. "Actually, I'd prefer that you wait. Let's talk before you read my piece, okay?"

"What's in the newspaper?" Will asked, following the couple into the homeless shelter.

"I don't know." Shirley went in with him. Goodness and Mercy were already inside. Goodness stood in the back of the room, with the newspaper spread open on one of the tabletops.

"Oh, no," she wailed and then slapped her hand over her mouth. Her eyes widened as she read the Lifestyle section.

"What is it?" Will asked, joining Goodness.

"It's Aren's restaurant review," Goodness explained. "The one for the place where he and Lucie dined Thursday night after the play."

"And . . ."

"Oh dear."

"What? What?" Mercy zoomed across the room. She tried to get a look herself but with Goodness, Shirley, and Will hovering over the newspaper she couldn't see a thing.

"What did Aren do, carry a recorder in his pocket?"

"What did he say?" Mercy demanded.

"He practically quoted every word Lucie said over dinner. The minute she reads this she'll know he's the food critic Eaton Well."

"Which is why he wants to talk to her before she reads the newspaper. Good heavens, why would he do such a thing?"

"Don't ask me."

A stunned silence followed. This was worse than bad. It would be disastrous to their budding relationship.

"Then it's our duty to make sure Lucie doesn't read that article."

"What can we do?" Shirley said, her wings sagging. "We've given Gabriel our word that we wouldn't interfere in their romance. The minute we do he'll know about it."

Mercy didn't know what the problem was, seeing that they'd already crossed the boundary line the night of the play. In fact, she was amazed they hadn't been called to task before now.

"Don't you think we're beyond worry about that now . . . after what happened at the play?" Mercy asked.

"Okay, okay, I know everyone is still upset with me about that camel. I'll admit I let matters get out of hand, but I did not, and I repeat, I did not, do anything to influence Aren and Lucie's feelings for each other."

"Me neither," Shirley reminded them. "Everything I did was on stage."

"That's right," Mercy said, and was cheered by the thought. While they had caused something of an Earthly sensation, it had been in innocent fun. For whatever reason, Gabriel hadn't mentioned the incident, and for that she counted her blessings. Her many blessings.

"Still, we must proceed with caution," Shirley said. "We don't want to cross the line but we need to keep Lucie in the dark until Aren has a chance to explain."

"Which means she can't read that article."

"It would be devastating to her," Will agreed.

"So we're all in agreement. We will take whatever measures necessary to keep the article out of Lucie's hands."

"But only the newspaper," Shirley said. "We won't involve ourselves in anything beyond that."

"Yes," each one said in turn.

"That will give Aren a chance to talk to her on Sunday, but if Lucie is upset with him after that, then what?" Will asked.

"Then she's upset."

"But what if . . ."

"We can't involve ourselves in happenstance," Mercy explained. "We'll deal with her reaction when the time comes."

"Seeing how I already botched up the timing," Will murmured, berating himself.

Shirley placed a gentle hand on his forearm. "It was a rookie mistake, don't be so hard on yourself. You should have witnessed some of the stunts Goodness and Mercy pulled when they first started work as Prayer Ambassadors."

"We all make mistakes," Mercy added. "Even Shirley."

"Oh, yes, I've made a few of my own," the former Guardian Angel admitted. "But with the help of my friends everything turned out fine."

"We'll set matters straight," Goodness assured

him, and they would. With God there were no accidents.

"Thank you so much for helping out," Lucie told Aren as they finished with the kitchen cleanup. Wendy washed dishes, Aren dried, and Lucie put everything back in its proper place.

The homeless had come and gone. Several commented that this was the best dinner they'd ever tasted.

"You do this on a regular basis?" Aren asked.

He sounded impressed, which pleased her, but actually she felt like the one who received after volunteering. "Our family has done this ever since I was a kid. Dad would join in, too. It just wouldn't be Christmas without doing something to help others. My parents were big on teaching my brother and me to give back."

"Did we wear you out?" Wendy asked, joining them.

Aren shook his head. "No. In fact I feel great. I should be exhausted but I'm not."

"I find it that way, too," Lucie told him. Seeing the faces of the men and women who came through the line had inspired her to do more, to be more, to invest more of herself in others. She thought about the staff at the restaurant and her friends with renewed appreciation. She thought about Aren, too, and how much she liked him and how grateful she was that he was back in her life.

"Lucie, you'd better leave now, sweetie, or you'll be late. I'll be right behind you once I finish up here."

Her mother was right. Impulsively she hugged Aren. Automatically his arms came around her and he held her close for the briefest of moments before reluctantly releasing her.

"Thank you again," she whispered close to his ear. "I'll always be grateful I met you."

"Always?" he asked, his eyes pleading with her.

The question seemed to hold within it another. One she didn't fully understand. "Yes," she assured him. If they were never to see each other again she would have no regrets. Although she was only beginning to know him, she felt strongly linked to him. Their relationship held such promise and the attraction remained strong and seemed to grow every time they were together.

Lucie looked into his eyes and saw doubt and regret. It shocked her, but unfortunately she didn't have time to ask or to figure it out.

Wendy brought Lucie her hat, coat, and scarf. The scarf was one of her favorites, mainly because her mother had knit it for her the Christmas before last. What made it special was that her mom had turned to knitting to help her grieve after the death of Lucie's father. This was the first piece Wendy had completed following her husband's death.

"I'll walk you outside," Aren offered.

"Oh, please do," Wendy added. "It's sometimes difficult getting a cab in this part of town."

"Mom, I'll be fine."

"Yes, you will, especially if Aren is with you. Now shoo."

Shaking her head, Lucie reached for her gloves and got her purse before joining Aren. She wasn't fooled. Her mother had used this as an excuse to give her more time with Aren, not that Lucie was complaining. She welcomed the opportunity.

Dusk had settled over the city. The streetlights had just come on. Because she'd been so busy with the demands of the restaurant Lucie hadn't taken much time to appreciate the season. Everything seemed so rushed. Her mother had set out a few Christmas decorations but their tree wasn't up and she had yet to start her shopping.

"I wish I had more time to spend with you," she told Aren as they walked to the closest intersection.

"It's fine, Lucie, don't stress over it."

"There's so much more I want to know about you."

He stepped halfway into the street and waved down a taxi. The first one sped past, but the second stopped.

Aren opened the door for her and Lucie climbed inside.

"I'll see you tomorrow," he told her, and leaning into the car, he gave her a quick kiss.

"I'll make a dinner you won't soon forget."

"You don't need to go to any trouble. What's important is being with you."

Lucie felt the same way. They would have the entire evening together, and the promise of that filled her with happy anticipation.

Aren closed the door and stepped back. She waved to him and, as was her custom, she placed her hand to her lips and then to the window.

After she gave the driver the address of Heavenly Delights, the taxi drove away, and Lucie settled into the seat. It was then that she noticed a copy of the *New York Gazette* on the seat next to her.

Chapter Twelve

An immediate sense of panic rose up in Mercy when she saw Lucie reach for the Saturday edition of the *New York Gazette* that rested next to her in the taxi.

"Quick," Goodness screeched, wagging her finger at Lucie. "Grab that newspaper."

Lucie reached for the paper and it wouldn't budge from the seat for the simple reason that Will sat on it. Tug as she might, the newspaper stayed exactly where it was.

"That's not going to work for long," Shirley cried, also in a panic. "Roll down the window and get rid of it."

Mercy reached over and quickly cranked the lever. Immediately a blast of cold air filled the cab.

Lucie gasped and reached over to roll up the window.

"Hey, lady, it's December. Roll up that blasted window before we both freeze."

"I'm trying. The handle seems to be stuck."

"Try harder."

Goodness reached for the newspaper and swirled it around the inside of the cab, which was no small feat, seeing how crowded it was with the four of them cramped inside the front and back seats plus the cabdriver and Lucie.

"You throw that newspaper out the window and I get charged with littering, then you're paying the fine, lady."

"I'm trying to get it," Lucie shouted back, but every time it came within her reach, Goodness jerked it away.

"Get rid of it," Mercy urged, doing her best to help and only adding to the mayhem.

"I don't want to litter," Shirley cried, wadding up the newspaper and stuffing it on the floorboards.

Lucie reached for it but before she could snatch it, Mercy grabbed the paper and shouted at her friend, "For the love of heaven, toss the thing. We can go back and pick it up later."

"Okay, okay."

Out the window the newspaper went, but as luck would have it, the pages landed at the feet of a policeman. He immediately leaped onto his motorcycle and gave chase, lights and siren blazing.

"Okay, lady, what did I tell you?" the cabbie grumbled. "You're paying the fine. I didn't have anything to do with this."

"Ah . . . I didn't litter, I swear. It just flew out of the cab all on its own."

"If that's your story then okay, but personally I

think you'd better come up with something a bit more original."

The taxi driver pulled to the side of the road and eased to a stop at the curb. The motorcycle cop parked directly behind him. He swung off his bike and walked directly to the side of the taxi. With his feet braced apart, and his thumbs tucked in his waistband, the officer waited for the taxi driver to roll down his window. The driver complied, but reluctantly.

"Hello, Officer. You need to talk to the passenger."

Lucie groaned inwardly and smiled weakly up at the patrolman. "Merry Christmas, Officer."

He stood tall and lean, and glared directly at her. "Would you like to explain yourself?"

"Ah . . ."

It appeared Lucie was at a loss for words.

The patrolman frowned and his face darkened. "Littering in the state of New York carries a hefty fine. Tossing a newspaper out a window is a safety hazard. That newspaper might have blinded a driver."

"Officer . . . I could make up a story, but what I'm telling you is the absolute truth. I wanted to read that newspaper but it felt like it was glued to the seat. Then the window rolled down without my doing anything. It was up and then all of a sudden it went down and I wasn't even close to that side of the cab. I thought the driver must have inadvertently pushed the button but when I looked over I saw it wasn't an automated window. Then he started yelling at me to roll it up but it wouldn't budge, and while I was trying to do that, the newspaper started making crazy circles in the vehicle and before I could grab it, it flew out the window."

"That's your story?"

"Yes," she said, "and every word of it is the truth, I swear."

"And you expect me to believe the window rolled down all on its own?"

"I swear I didn't touch it. It came down all by itself."

He glared back at her and shook his head as though her story was completely unbelievable.

"Do you honestly think I'd purposely litter right in front of you?" Lucie asked.

"Lady," the cabdriver called back to her, "it's better not to argue; just take the ticket and let's get out of here."

The police officer's frown darkened even more.

"Actually I was looking forward to reading that newspaper," Lucie continued. "A friend of mine has an article in it."

The officer looked at the driver and then back at Lucie. "Well, you're in luck because I saved it." He left and returned to his motorcycle.

"He's got that and a ticket just for you," the cabbie told her. "And it's your fine, lady. I warned you."

"So you keep reminding me," Lucie muttered.

The officer returned and handed her the newspaper.

"Can I plead for mercy?" Lucie asked, folding her hands and gazing up at him. "It was a freak accident. I'm sure nothing like this will ever happen again."

He hesitated and then nodded. "Okay, I'll let you off this time. Just make sure you don't have any other freak accidents."

"I'll do my best."

"I'd have an easier time believing you if you rolled up that window," he said, shaking his head.

"I tried earlier but it was stuck."

"Try again."

Naturally it rolled up without the least bit of effort. Lucie groaned with frustration. "I realize this makes everything I told you sound like a lie, but it was the truth. Every word."

"Can we go now?" the cabbie asked.

"Go and sin no more," the officer said, looking directly past Lucie.

The taxi driver didn't need any encouragement. He eased back into traffic and took off at an accelerated pace, tossing Lucie back against the cushioned seat.

Mercy expelled her breath and grabbed both Shirley and Goodness by the arm. "Do . . . you know who . . . that was?" she stuttered.

"Yes," Will answered for them. "It was an officer of the law."

"No, it wasn't," Mercy said, shaking so badly several feathers threatened to fall from her wings. "That was Gabriel. He looked straight at me."

"Gabriel?" Goodness slapped her hand over her mouth. "How do you know?"

"Go and sin no more? What New York patrolman would say something like that?"

"He knows it was us causing Lucie those problems."

"The newspaper, the newspaper," Will cried. "Lucie's reading the newspaper."

Sure enough, Lucie had it open to the front page and was scanning the contents, seeking out Aren's name.

"Oh, no," Will muttered. "After everything we went through . . ."

Mercy quieted him with a single glance. "Not to worry. It's Friday's edition."

"Friday? You mean we went through all that for a day-old newspaper?" Shirley collapsed onto the seat next to Lucie. "I'm too old for this kind of excitement." She pressed her hand over her heart.

"It wasn't Friday's edition that got tossed out the window," Will said quickly. "I saw the date before I sat down and it was definitely the Saturday edition."

"Then that really was Gabriel," Shirley whispered. "I had no idea he intervened with matters on Earth."

"Me either . . . I've never known him to do anything like that before." Mercy remained shaken. "You know what this means, don't you?" she asked her fellow Prayer Ambassadors.

"Huh?"

"Tell us."

"It means Gabriel doesn't want Lucie reading that paper before Aren talks to her either. He's giving us his tacit permission to do whatever is necessary to see that doesn't happen."

"Gabriel?" Goodness repeated as though shocked. "Do you honestly believe that?"

"It makes sense, otherwise he would have pulled us from Earth so fast our heads would be spinning."

"He might clip our wings yet," Goodness pointed out.

"Oh dear, oh dear," Shirley cried. "Listen, the three of you go on without me." She pressed the back of her hand against her forehead. "I don't know that I can take this pressure any longer. I think I might have bent my wing flapping around the inside of this cab."

"Relax," Mercy said, taking her friend's hand and patting it gently. "Take in deep breaths and you'll be fine in a couple of minutes."

"Can I do anything?" Will asked, looking concerned.

"No, no, everything should be okay in a couple hundred light-years," Shirley reassured him.

"Deep breaths," Goodness repeated. "Take in deep breaths."

"Oh, I do feel better."

The cab pulled to a stop outside Heavenly Delights and Lucie paid the fare and climbed out. She paused on the sidewalk and glanced down the street. Mercy's gaze followed Lucie's and she gasped, drawing in a deep breath.

"What is it?" Goodness demanded.

"There's a newsstand down the street," Mercy said and shot out of the cab.

Goodness and Will followed.

"Don't leave me," Shirley pleaded and reluctantly followed.

Lucie walked down to the stand, saw the newspaper, and opened her purse, digging inside her wallet for the correct change.

"Now what?" Will asked, glancing from one to the other.

"This is a piece of cake," Mercy insisted. She sat on top of the pile and crossed her legs, while the proprietor dealt with another customer.

Lucie set the proper change on the counter and tried to pick up the paper. Sure enough it wouldn't budge. She jerked again, harder this time. Nothing. The man at the stand was dealing with two youths who had apparently been causing problems and completely ignored her.

Mercy crossed her arms and looked pleased with herself.

Then Lucie kicked the papers and off Mercy flew, butt first onto the sidewalk. Thankfully Will quickly replaced her.

Lucie gasped and fell back two steps as if she wasn't sure what had just happened. She took her purse strap and wrapped it over her shoulder and tried again.

Will held fast.

Another cab pulled up to the restaurant and after a couple of moments, Wendy climbed out. She stood outside the entrance to the restaurant and watched as her daughter tried once again with no success.

"Lucie?"

Lucie turned to see her mother standing outside of Heavenly Delights.

"I thought you'd be here ages before me," her mother said, joining her.

"Mom, I want to read Aren's article, but I've had nothing but problems. You would hardly believe what's been happening."

"How frustrating." Wendy glanced up at the proprietor.

"If I didn't know better I'd think I'm losing my mind. I had the most outrageous thing happen in the cab, too."

"Come, you can tell me all about it later, but right now we need to get into the restaurant."

Lucie hesitated, kicked the stack one last time, and then joined her mother.

"I'm sure we'll find a used newspaper inside," Wendy was saying. "You know how people are always leaving those sorts of things behind."

Lucie agreed. "I know it sounds nuts, but it's like everything is working against me."

As soon as they turned away, Shirley released a heaving sigh. "That was close."

Mercy barely heard her friend and pointed at their young apprentice. "Will, get into the restaurant and make sure there are no Saturday newspapers to be found."

"Got it." He shot off like a rocket.

"I'll help," Goodness insisted and zoomed after him.

"Shirley?" Mercy asked. Her friend looked pale. "Do you want to return to heaven?" she asked.

The former Guardian Angel's eyes widened. "And miss all this craziness? I don't think so."

Mercy smiled.

"Besides, I don't want to face Gabriel all alone."

For that Mercy didn't blame her. The two quickly joined Goodness and Will. Mercy was surprised by how busy the restaurant was this early in the evening. Lucie and her mother should be pleased.

And she was right, because Mercy overheard Wendy say to Lucie a few minutes later, "Every table is booked and we have several people on a wait list."

Lucie glanced up from her workstation. Catherine, who'd attended culinary school with Lucie and Jazmine and filled in for Lucie on occasion and on her day off, smiled, too.

"That negative review might have done you more good than harm," Catherine said.

Lucie frowned. "I doubt that."

"Every table, Lucie. That's high praise all on its own."

"Yes, I suppose it is, and while the review might not have hurt us—thanks to all our loyal customers—I still don't think I could ever forgive Eaton Well for that original review."

"Lucie, that's not like you," Wendy said, and seemed surprised.

"Mom, think about it. The sarcasm just wasn't necessary. I would never want to associate with anyone who could write something that cutting and cruel. He seemed to find pleasure in tearing down the chef, which just so happened to be me."

"You know these critics. They work at being clever."

"At other people's expense. Well, I, for one, don't think it's amusing. These are people's lives . . . their everything."

"Oh, Lucie, you need to be more forgiving," her mother chastised.

"Nope, not in this instance. It's not going to happen."

———

Mercy froze and looked to her friends. "Did you hear that?"

All three nodded in unison.

"We have our work cut out for us," Goodness whispered.

"Oh, yes, we do," Will agreed.

Chapter Thirteen

Aren's cell chirped as he sat, crashed out, in front of the television. Glancing at Caller ID, he saw that it was his sister, Josie.

"You up for a movie?" she asked.

"Thanks but no thanks. I'm exhausted."

"Just from cleaning your apartment?" she teased.

"No, Lucie phoned and asked if I'd give her a hand."

"Doing what?"

"If I told you, I doubt you'd believe me."

"Try me," Josie said, and sounded amused.

"We served two hundred fifty meals at the Salvation Army homeless shelter."

"You?" She did nothing to disguise her surprise.

"Yes, me, and don't sound so shocked."

"You've never done anything like that before."

His sister was right, Aren hadn't. He'd thought about it, but wasn't sure how to go about volunteering. All he'd ever done was stick a few dollars in the red bucket at Christmastime. That was as far as his generosity stretched. He made routine donations to a number of worthy causes, but he'd never gotten personally involved. His need to give back had been satisfied by that comfortable barrier of a check stuffed in an envelope and tossed into the mailbox.

"Apparently Lucie and her family volunteer at the shelter every year."

"Really?" Even Josie sounded impressed. "How'd it go?"

Aren propped his feet on the ottoman. Leaning back, he closed his eyes as a rush of good feelings washed over him. "The truth is, if Lucie had told me why she needed my help I would probably have found an excuse to beg off. I feel bad and all about people living on the streets, but that's about as far as my thought process goes."

"Yeah, me too. It's sort of overwhelming, isn't it?"

"Yes, with such a huge problem what can one person do?"

"Right," she agreed.

"Well, I found out. I can do a lot. I can dish up two hundred fifty servings of beef gravy and green beans. I can smile and wish everyone in line a Merry Christmas. And when I finish serving I can go around and ask if they need anything more to drink."

"You did all that?"

"I did, plus I helped load up the dishwasher and

get everything set up for the next meal, and while I'm tired, I'm feeling good, too."

"Wow, and you say Lucie does this every year?"

"It's tradition for her family. Apparently they volunteer several days in December. Lucie and her mother did the cooking, and if that wasn't enough, Lucie had to hurry in order to get to the restaurant."

"She's working an entire shift after spending all afternoon at the shelter?"

"So it seems."

His sister hesitated. "She's special, isn't she?"

Aren didn't need to think twice. After his failed marriage, he'd been gun-shy when it came to relationships. It was bad enough that Katie had taken up with an old lover, but what really hurt beyond the deception was how he'd found out. Aren had walked in on Katie in bed with her lover . . . in the house and bed Aren shared with his wife. The scene that followed was one that would stick in his mind for the rest of his life. He'd filed for divorce and Katie actually seemed grateful to end the marriage.

The worst of it was the psychological ramifications. He felt like someone who'd taken a bad spill down a flight of stairs and forever after clung to the railing, no matter how few steps there were.

"I know you like Lucie," Josie continued.

He couldn't deny it. "I've finally met the woman I've been hoping to find. Lucie gives me hope that I can fall in love again. She makes me believe I can trust another woman."

Josie expelled her breath in a deep sigh. "Katie really did a number on you, didn't she?"

"You could say that."

"But, Aren, Lucie doesn't know the full truth about you."

That was the one stumbling block in his way. He hoped he'd be able to clear the air on Sunday either right before dinner or after. "She will soon enough, and if she's half the woman I think she is, then she'll be willing to look beyond that review."

"I don't know what went wrong that first night at the restaurant," Josie added.

"I don't either." Still, Aren would stick by his review of the dish he was served. As far as he was concerned it was completely inedible.

"I've been to the restaurant several times now," Josie continued, "and the food is always incredible. I just don't know what happened that night."

"I don't know either, and I agree with you. Lucie is exceptionally gifted in the kitchen."

"She didn't read Eaton Well's column in today's paper, did she?"

"No, thank heaven."

"What happened? I thought your review was scheduled for next Saturday."

"I did, too. Apparently Sandy Markus decided to put it in this week following the article I wrote about what happened at *Angels at Christmas*. It makes sense seeing that I casually mention that we went to that restaurant following the play."

"She might have warned you."

"She might have told me?" Aren snickered. "Sandy has a paper to publish and what happens to me when one of my pieces is printed means nothing to her. In her mind I should be grateful for my job. And I am grateful. This has been a wonderful opportunity for me."

Josie hesitated for a moment and then asked, "You sure I can't talk you into a movie?"

"Not tonight, sis."

"Okay, well, I guess I'll head to the theater on my own, then."

Josie did sound a bit down. These days she rarely mentioned Jack, but Aren knew the breakup remained fresh in his sister's mind although it'd happened over a year ago. "What about asking one of your friends?"

"It's December; they're all busy with shopping and family. Such is the life of a single woman."

"You ever hear from Jack?" Aren ventured. His question was followed by a short, uncomfortable silence.

"Never," she said without elaborating.

His sister quickly changed the subject. She wasn't interested in dating again, it seemed. Seeing how sensitive Josie was about Jack, Aren regretted bringing up the other man.

They ended the conversation and, sometime later,

Aren heated up a bowl of canned soup and made himself a peanut butter and jelly sandwich. He couldn't help thinking about Lucie and how tired she must be. He decided to call her in the morning and offer to take her out to dinner instead of having her cook. She needed a break. He hoped they would have some privacy to discuss the article and his role at the newspaper.

It was after eleven and Aren was watching TV when his doorbell chimed. His first thought was that it might be Lucie, but after checking the peephole he saw it wasn't.

Opening the door, he found Josie standing there, pale and obviously upset. "Hey, what's up?"

She ignored the question. "Can I come in for a minute?"

"Of course." He ushered his sister inside and closed the door after her.

Josie collapsed onto his sofa and then sat on the very edge of the cushion. Reaching for a wadded-up tissue, she focused her attention on shredding it into small pieces.

"That must have been one heck of a movie," he said, aiming for a comical slant.

"I . . . I didn't go."

"Why not?"

Instead of answering, she scrambled through her purse for a fresh tissue and then dabbed at the corner of each eye before blowing her nose. She sat up straighter and then squared her shoulders. "Guess who I ran into?" she asked, in a flippant tone.

"I'm guessing it wasn't Santa and his elves."

Her eyes narrowed as she glared at him. "No. I ran into Jack. Thankfully, I don't think he saw me."

"Jack who?"

"You're not being funny, Aren. This isn't a time for jokes. Can't you see I'm upset?"

"All right, all right, sorry. So you saw Jack."

"He wasn't alone," she added. By now her spine was as stiff as a mop handle. Pride, it appeared, was great for proper posture.

"Jack was with another woman?" Oh, that must have hurt.

Josie nodded and, relaxing her shoulders, reached for a fresh tissue. "Jack and this other woman were laughing and teasing each other, having the time of their lives. And here I was by myself, standing in line for a movie ticket."

"Oh, Josie, I'm so sorry." Aren wished now that he had gone with her, if for no other reason than moral support.

"I feel like such a loser."

Aren sat down next to her and gave her arm a gentle squeeze. "You know that's not true."

"Maybe so, but that's the way I felt. Here I am lonely and miserable and Jack—"

"And Jack has gotten on with his life." Aren finished for her.

Josie made a weak effort to laugh. "Big time."

"Was she pretty?"

His sister slammed him with a look that would have melted kryptonite. "What do you think?"

"Drop-dead gorgeous," he muttered. Aren knew the feeling. Katie's lover was a bodybuilder with muscles—speaking of kryptonite—Superman would have envied. The strongest muscles in Aren's body were in his fingers from all the typing and texting. Compared to the man Katie dumped him for, Aren felt like the ninety-eight-pound weakling.

"I'm sorry, sis." He did commiserate with her. "Can I get you anything?"

Josie raised her head. "What have you got?"

Unfortunately Aren had never been much of a drinker, so he didn't keep alcohol in the apartment. "Beer, I think. If I had chocolate I'd offer that."

"I don't know, Aren. The way I feel right now there aren't enough chocolate chip cookies in the world to get me through this."

"So you still love him?" Actually the answer was fairly obvious, at least to him.

From the way she hesitated Aren could see that she held strong feelings for Jack, although she was reluctant to admit it. "I think I must. I thought I'd be able to put him out of my mind, but I was wrong."

"Have you thought about contacting him?" That seemed an obvious solution to Aren.

Josie stared down at her hands and the crumbled tissues there. "Actually, I almost did tonight . . .

right before I called you. That would have been a real hoot, wouldn't it? Jack would have gotten a kick out of that, now that he's dating Miss Universe."

"Stop. You're no slouch, Josie. You're smart and attractive and well educated and—"

"Sure," she scoffed, "you'd say that, seeing that we swam out of the same gene pool."

Aren laughed. "I mean it. The way I see it, you've got two choices: you could either attempt to patch things up with Jack, or you could get on with your own life. The choice is yours."

"Well, I'm not going to chase after Jack, that's for sure."

"Then you don't love him. You simply don't want him to find anyone else. You want him to pine after you the rest of his life."

Her gaze shot to his and for a second she looked stricken by his comment. "That's not the least bit true. I do care."

"No, you don't, especially if you're willing to walk away."

"He's found someone else," Josie argued.

"You don't know that for sure," he countered just as swiftly. "And if he did, so what? You care, too."

"So what? Clearly you don't understand the situation. I saw Jack with her and I can tell you right now, he wasn't thinking about me the way I have been thinking about him."

Aren figured they could argue about this all night and it wouldn't do any good.

"All I'm saying, sis, is that if you have such strong feelings then let him know. If you don't, then let it go. Do what you can to learn from the experience and walk away."

Josie stood and hung her head as she seemed to consider his advice. After a moment or two, she whispered, "I've got too much pride to reach out to Jack . . . eventually I'll meet someone else, too."

Aren understood the pride issue all too well. "Yes, you will," he said in as reassuring a tone as he could manage, and he hoped that was true.

"Did you hear that?" Will asked Goodness. The two had left Mercy and Shirley with Lucie and her mother. Their friends kept a diligent watch on Lucie to keep her and the Eaton Well column separated from each other. Will and Goodness had gone to check on Aren.

"We've got to help poor Josie," Will said, feeling dreadful over her failed romance.

"We can't. It's strictly forbidden."

"But she's in love and miserable and hurting. Isn't that part of our mission, to comfort those in pain?"

"We're Prayer Ambassadors, Will. Someone has to pray for her first."

"Can't she pray?"

"Of course, but apparently she hasn't."

"Why not?"

Goodness shrugged. "It's funny. Some humans are prayer warriors and then there are others who only pray when they're desperate or badly in need of divine intervention. Then they urgently cry out to God for help."

"Do we answer those frantic prayers?" Will asked.

"We do what we can on short notice."

Will watched as Josie buttoned up her coat and headed into the cold night. The festive feel of the holidays was all around her, but Aren's sister didn't appear to notice. She kept her head lowered and her shoulders hunched forward against the cold and wind.

At the corner, she stopped at a red light, reached inside her purse, and took out her cellphone. For a long time all she did was stare at it; then she glanced at her watch, sighed, and tossed it back into her purse.

"Do you think she was going to call Jack?" Will asked.

"Don't know. We should get back and check on Aren."

Will glanced over his shoulder. "Can I follow Josie to make sure she gets home okay?"

Goodness bit into her lower lip. "All right, but don't let Mercy or Shirley know that I said you could."

"Okay."

"And Will?"

"Yes?"

Goodness tapped her foot impatiently. "You've really got to get a tougher skin when it comes to dealing with humans. God granted them free will. If we become involved in his or her lives it can get messy."

"But God loves them."

"He does very much. It pains Him to watch them make wrong choices, but He's determined to let each one make his or her own decisions."

"Including Josie."

"Including Josie," Goodness echoed.

"And Aren and Lucie."

"Exactly." All Goodness could do was hope everything turned out well for the newsman and the chef.

Chapter Fourteen

"You must be exhausted." Lucie's mother followed her into her bedroom after her shift at the restaurant.

"You, too, Mom." Her mother had worked nearly as many hours as Lucie despite her medical condition. Thankfully Aren had been able to help with the serving earlier in the day. He'd been wonderful, really wonderful. He wouldn't allow either of them to lift anything and had carted all the heavy pots and serving dishes back and forth. As soon as he had arrived, Aren had dug right in, lending a helping hand.

It was far more than his willingness to serve that touched her heart. Aren had been terrific with the men and women, chatting with them, making them feel welcome, asking questions, making conversation. He'd been willing to listen when so many others had looked the other way, and he'd been great with the children, too.

"I am tired, but I wasn't the one slaving over a hot stove all night."

"Mom, I love what I do."

Her mother hugged her and then went off to her own bedroom. Sammy remained patiently at Lucie's side, waiting for her and willing to follow wherever she led.

Lucie took a long hot shower and dressed for bed. Sunday afternoon she'd cook dinner for Aren and she planned to make it a meal he would long remember. Years ago her mother had told her the way to a man's heart was through his stomach. She wanted Aren's heart. Despite all the demands on her time, the responsibility of making the restaurant a success, Lucie couldn't help falling in love with Aren. He was easy to love. Her head and her heart were full as she drifted off to sleep.

Her dreams that night were filled with Aren. She woke to the smell of freshly brewed coffee.

"Morning, sweetheart," Wendy said when Lucie staggered into the kitchen, rubbing the sleep from her eyes.

Automatically her mother poured Lucie a cup of coffee. "We've got an hour before church this morning. Advent is my favorite time of year. I just love singing Christmas carols."

"Me too." With so much to do on her day off, Lucie was tempted to skip worship service. It would be easy to offer her mother an excuse. She didn't and was glad because the service was inspiring.

If she lacked Christmas spirit, working with the homeless at the Salvation Army and attending church had given her more than an ample supply.

After church, Lucie and Wendy dragged out the Christmas tree decorations from the storage space in the apartment basement. She hoped Aren wouldn't mind helping her set up the tree later. It would be fun and romantic.

Before Lucie made one final trip to the basement for the last load of decorations, her mother announced she had made plans for the afternoon. She was going shopping with a friend and they might take in a movie afterward. Lucie wasn't fooled. This was a gift of time alone with Aren.

On the way up the stairs, Lucie ran into her neighbor. "Merry Christmas, Mrs. Sullivan," she said cheerfully. Her mood was high, filled with happy anticipation for her afternoon with Aren.

"Merry Christmas, Lucie." Her elderly neighbor was hauling a box of trash to the recycling bin.

"Oh, is that Saturday's newspaper?" she asked, eyeing the date on the paper on the very top of the box.

"It is."

"Would you mind if I read it?"

"Be my guest."

Lucie grabbed the newspaper and stuffed it under her arm as she raced up the stairs. She was anxious to look for Aren's name. He'd asked her to wait to read it, which seemed a little silly. It would be the first time he had a byline and she was proud of him.

"I got Saturday's newspaper," Lucie called out as soon as she returned to the apartment. Setting down the last box of ornaments, she pulled out a kitchen chair and spread out the newspaper. After going through every section twice she couldn't find Aren's name anywhere.

"It's not here," she said, disappointment coating her words. "Not the way I expected, at least."

"How do you mean?" her mother asked.

"Well, he mentioned that he wrote a short piece about the play we saw and what happened but there's no real byline there, just a note to check out the restaurant review, but that doesn't make any sense."

"Did you read the restaurant review?" Her mother sounded as disappointed as Lucie.

"No," Lucie admitted.

"Does he write for sports?" her mother asked, as if Lucie had reached for the wrong section.

"No . . . actually, he's never mentioned what he writes." In fact, now that she thought about it, Aren had always been rather secretive about what he did for the newspaper.

"Well, check out the restaurant review," her mother suggested.

As it was, Lucie was confused. "He couldn't have anything to do with that. The review is written by Eaton Well."

"Then don't read it," her mother said, shaking her head. "Every time you even glance at his column you get upset."

"And rightly so. The man is an idiot."

"Lucie, you shouldn't say that."

"I can't help it, Mom. Eaton Well nearly ruined us. Oh, and look," she said, pointing to the column. "Sure enough he's reviewing the same restaurant where Aren and I had dinner last Thursday night." She picked up the paper and skimmed through the article. Not more than two inches into the column and her fingers tightened, crumpling the edges of the newspaper.

"Lucie, I told you not to read his review. It upsets you every time."

She swallowed hard, closed her eyes, and set the newspaper back down on the table. Slowly she came to her feet as a tight knot formed in her throat.

"Was it another negative review?" her mother asked.

"It was fair," she said, her voice cracking slightly as the realization hit her. Aren was Eaton Well. This was the reason he hadn't wanted her to read the paper until after they spoke. He intended on telling her that he'd been the one who wrote that horrible review of Heavenly Delights. He hadn't known at the time that she was the chef who'd prepared his meal. The sole had been one of her signature dishes, one she was most proud to add to the menu. And he'd panned it with language so harsh the sting lingered in her mind even now, all these weeks later.

"Lucie, are you all right?" Wendy asked.

"Yes, Mom." She was on her feet, although she didn't know what she intended to do or where she thought she would go. It felt as if the room had suddenly shrunk to half its size, as though the walls were closing in on her. She had nowhere to hide; nowhere to run.

"What time will Aren be here?" her mother asked.

"Ah . . . I don't recall." Her head started to spin. Aren would be at the apartment soon. It would be impossible to look at him now, knowing what she did.

"Janice is stopping by to pick me up in an hour. Are you sure you don't want any help decorating the tree?"

The tree. Lucie had completely forgotten she'd agreed to decorate the Christmas tree. A task she'd been looking forward to doing with Aren. Now it would be impossible. "I'll get the tree up, Mom, no problem."

"If Aren has something else in mind, then don't bother, okay?"

"Sure." She walked to one end of the kitchen and then back, lost in a fog that refused to clear. What she needed to do was think and that would be out of the question if Aren was with her.

Aren. Aren was Eaton Well.

Lucie had trouble wrapping her mind around what she should have figured out long ago.

"Lucie, are you all right? You've gone quite pale. Are you sure you're feeling okay? I could stay home, if you wanted."

"No . . . I'm fine. Go and have fun . . . enjoy your day."

"I will." Her mother hummed as she buzzed about the room, sorting out the stacks on the kitchen countertop and then addressing a few Christmas cards while she waited for her friend to arrive.

Lucie bided her time until her mother left. Then, gathering her resolve, she reached for her phone. Of primary importance was to find an excuse to keep Aren away. She needed to think, to absorb what she'd learned, figure out what to do.

Aren answered on the first ring and when he found out it was her, he said, "Hello. I was just on my way out the door."

"I'm glad I caught you, then." Lucie did her best to sound as though nothing was wrong.

"What's up?"

In a flash, it came to her what to do. "I've been doing some thinking."

Something in her voice must have betrayed her feelings because Aren suddenly went quiet. Lucie could hear the background noise. The sound of an elevator opening. The rushing sound of the doors closing and then nothing.

"Thinking about what?" he asked, sounding strained and uncertain, as though testing her.

"Us. When we met all those months ago, I told you that my life was crazy busy with the restaurant and all. The timing to get involved with someone couldn't be worse for me. I realize now that nothing has really changed."

"In other words you want to cool it."

"Yes."

He didn't say anything for a long time and then in a soft voice, he asked, "You saw the article, didn't you?"

"Yes." She wasn't going to lie to him.

"And now you hate me?"

"No." Lucie could never hate Aren. "I . . . need to take a step back and reevaluate our relationship. You aren't the person I thought you were."

"You're wrong, Lucie."

"You were cruel and mean in the review you wrote about Heavenly Delights. Eaton Well isn't a kind person . . . he thinks he's being clever and he isn't. He uses words to cut people down . . . what you wrote about Heavenly Delights was unjustifiable and—"

"I was honest," he said, cutting into her short tirade.

"My cooking is that bad? You're telling me that the effort and investment my mother and I put into this restaurant was a waste of time and that we deserve to fail?"

"I didn't write anything even close to that."

"You might as well have."

He didn't respond, which was just as well. Arguing the point would do no good.

"You didn't answer my question," she continued. "Tell me now and be truthful. Did the sole actually taste that bad?"

Again Aren hesitated as if looking for a way around the truth, his truth. "Everyone has an off day now and again."

"That bad?" she repeated, louder this time, more insistent.

A heartbeat passed before he answered. "Yes, that bad."

"I see," she choked out. "That tells me everything."

"Lucie, you're being unreasonable and unfair."

"I'm being unfair? Well, if that isn't calling the kettle black I don't know what is."

"Okay, fine, if you don't want to see me again—"

"You should have told me who you really are long before now," she argued.

"I couldn't. My contract doesn't allow me to tell you outright, so I did the best I could. I was as honest as possible. I told you the only way I could by quoting you in my column. I knew the minute you read the review you would know. You can't fault me for misleading you."

He was right, and while she wanted to argue with him, she couldn't. That didn't change the fact that he was the man who'd been willing to ruin her and her mother's investment. Lucie couldn't overlook that.

"I understand that you did your best not to deceive me . . ." she began. That was key to him, she realized, because he'd been deceived by his wife. Nevertheless it didn't alter the fact that he was who he was.

"But . . ." He said it before she had the chance.

"But it isn't working, Aren. It just isn't working."

"I don't believe you."

"Excuse me?" she flared. Lucie hadn't expected this to be easy. What she found difficult was the way he challenged her. She anticipated Aren would respond with angry pride and defend his actions. Instead he sounded reasonable and unruffled, making it all the harder to do what needed to be done.

"You heard me loud and clear. Our relationship is working and that frightens you. You've come to trust me and when I found fault with your cooking you couldn't take the criticism."

"You're so off base it isn't even funny." This wasn't about pride. The problem was she was falling for Aren and falling hard. The man she didn't feel she could trust was Eaton Well and to discover they were one and the same made it necessary to reassess their relationship.

"I doubt I'm that far off base," he returned, sounding completely unruffled. "You're afraid."

"Okay, I'm afraid. I'll admit it."

He paused as if he hadn't expected her to own up to her own fears.

"What are you really saying, Lucie? Do you want to take a breather or do you want to cut off our relationship entirely?"

"I . . . think it would be best if we didn't see each other."

"Ever again?"

Lucie closed her eyes and tightened her hold on her cellphone. Already it was pressed against her ear so hard it would leave an indentation. "I . . . don't know." Now wasn't the time to make that kind of decision.

"Leaving me dangling seems rather unfair, don't you think?"

"Yes," she had to agree.

"Then decide. If you want to take a break then let's do it. We can meet again in a month or two and talk then."

"I . . . need longer."

"Three months?"

"I don't know." She closed her eyes.

Aren chuckled softly and without humor. "I believe I'm getting the message. You want me completely out of your life but you don't have the courage to say it."

Lucie didn't know if that was true or not. "I . . . don't know what to say. I need time."

"Then take all the time you need. But I'm sticking by my review. I don't know what happened that night with the sole, but in my opinion it should never have been served.

"You had over three hundred patrons who strongly disagreed with me and I had the opportunity to dine a second time at Heavenly Delights, and I was glad I did because the meal was wonderful. I wrote a rave review. I gave you another chance."

"I know," she whispered, feeling dreadful. He had written a positive review but that was after he knew she was the chef.

"It's a shame you're unwilling to do the same for me."

Before she could say another word, Aren whispered, "Good-bye, Lucie," and hung up.

"How did Lucie get that newspaper?" Mercy cried, watching events unfold from the Brooklyn skyline above Lucie's apartment. "Who was assigned to watch her?"

Will reluctantly raised his hand. "She was in the basement. I didn't even see who gave it to her. I'm so sorry . . . and now everything is ruined, and once again it's all my fault."

Gabriel appeared beside them, arriving unexpectedly and with little fanfare. "So how is the romance developing between Lucie and Aren?" he asked, although Mercy strongly suspected he already knew the answer.

No one seemed inclined to respond.

"She just told him she doesn't want to see him," Shirley muttered. "And it's all our fault."

"We messed with her sauce for the fish and that upset God's plan," Will admitted.

"That's the problem," Gabriel said and folded his arms over his massive chest. "And it's a big one. There's a very good reason Prayer Ambassadors are asked not to get involved with matters on Earth. When you do, things can get messy."

"Real messy," Shirley agreed. "And I'm to blame."

"I'm at fault, too," Goodness confessed.

"We're all guilty," Mercy chimed in, and the worst of it was they'd led young Will astray as well.

"Can we fix it?" Will asked eagerly.

Gabriel looked from one to the other. "I think it might be best if you left it alone and let Lucie and Aren sort this out for themselves," he suggested.

"But will they?" Mercy pleaded, needing to know. It grieved her that two people who seemed so right together would allow this to stand between them. She wanted to help but knew she dared not.

"What happens is up to them," Gabriel said, and then he did something completely out of character. Gabriel gently patted Mercy's shoulder. "We aren't meant to understand why humans make the decisions they do. It's all about free will."

"But Aren and Lucie are so right for each other," Will argued.

"Are they?" Gabriel posed the question.

Unfortunately the answer was one Shirley, Goodness, Mercy, and Will didn't know.

Chapter Fifteen

"Why the glum look?" Josie asked when Aren met his sister Monday morning. "I thought you spent the day with Lucie and she cooked you dinner."

"I didn't go."

"What?" Josie nearly stumbled into the man standing in front of her in the Starbucks line. "Why not? Being with Lucie was all you could talk about on Saturday."

That wasn't entirely true. The one doing the talking had been his sister. Josie had been bemoaning the sorry state of her life after she saw Jack. Aren wished now he'd been a little more sympathetic seeing that he was currently the one on the receiving end of rejection.

"It's over between us," he stated matter-of-factly, as if it was of little consequence. In reality, Lucie was all he'd thought about from the moment he'd disconnected the call. She'd made her feelings clear. No matter what he said, Lucie wasn't going to change her mind. She wanted a breather, or so she said, but he didn't need a crystal ball to read her mind. Lucie didn't want anything more to do with him, only she hadn't been strong enough to say it.

One look told him Josie had figured out what had happened. "Lucie read the column, didn't she?"

The Starbucks line moved forward and so did they. "Yeah, and sweet as she appears, she doesn't have a forgiving nature."

Josie frowned. "Are you going to leave it like that?"

Aren's gaze shot to his sister. "I don't have any choice."

"Hold on just a minute. Weren't you the one who lectured me about Jack and pride and telling me that if I was really in love with him I couldn't take our breakup sitting down?"

"I said all that?" Aren wanted to eat those words now, seeing that they were coming back to bite him.

"That and more."

"Did you take them to heart?" He knew she hadn't and now, seeing the situation from her side, he understood why.

"As a matter of fact I did." Seeing that it was her turn in line, Josie stepped to the counter and ordered for the both of them.

Aren hadn't expected his sister to buy his coffee. He'd done it for her recently and apparently this was payback.

The barista handed them each a grande coffee and Josie paid with a swipe of her debit card. They started toward the subway when Aren pushed for more information.

"You contacted Jack?"

"Not yet, but I thought long and hard about what you said. You're right, Aren. I have to face the fact that I do care for Jack. What I need to decide is if the pain I felt seeing him with another woman was real or if I was simply jealous and angry that he's recovered enough to date someone new."

"What did you decide?"

"I haven't . . . not yet."

Aren shook his head. They were certainly a pair, hurting and broken and both unwilling to let go of their pride. "I'm beginning to think I'd be better off concentrating on my career," he told his sister. "It's best if I avoid relationships completely."

"Don't be silly. You want a wife and family."

"Who says?" he argued.

"I do. You'd make a wonderful husband and father. You can't let a little bad luck stand in your way."

"It's more than bad luck. This is karma. Every relationship I've had—or been close to having—has gone down in flames."

"Not true. What about Mary Jane Milton. She was crazy about you in high school."

"I saw her at our last high school reunion. Married, three kids, and another on the way."

"See, you didn't act fast enough."

"I was seventeen."

They came to the subway and his sister paused. "Meet me for dinner," Josie insisted.

"I'm working late," he muttered. He knew she wanted to help, but this thing with Lucie was fresh in his mind and he preferred to take a couple of days to lick his wounds.

"Fine, call me when you're finished and we'll meet somewhere convenient."

"I . . ."

"Don't argue with me," she said and started down the stairs. Halfway down, she paused and looked back. "Don't disappoint me, Aren."

It didn't look as if he'd be able to get out of this easily, so he decided to make the best of it. Dinner with his sister should be safe enough.

Thankfully Aren was busy from the moment he walked into work. The distractions helped keep his mind off Lucie. He ate lunch at his desk, swallowing his sandwich of roast beef with horseradish sauce and a cup of hot coffee. By six he was tired and out of sorts. Dinner with Josie held little appeal, seeing that she was sure to lecture him. Aren wished now he'd kept his mouth shut when it came to dishing out advice, especially now that Josie was sure to give it back to him.

Being a dutiful brother, he called her as promised.

"You hungry?" she asked.

Aren had to think about it. "I suppose."

"Great. Meet me at the Italian place I told you about." She gave him the cross streets.

"Are you buying?"

"Yes, so don't argue."

Aren realized giving her an excuse wouldn't do any good, so he capitulated. He didn't have any trouble catching a taxi and did his best to ignore the festive mood that seemed to permeate the city. He didn't want to think about Christmas. He had other matters on his mind. Not matters, he admitted, Lucie. He tried not to think about their painful conversation but it kept repeating itself in his mind. Bottom line: Lucie didn't feel she could trust him. She claimed she didn't know him.

Josie was waiting outside the restaurant when Aren's taxi pulled to a stop at the curb.

"This is one of my favorite restaurants in the entire city," Josie said as way of greeting. "Their red sauce is the best I've ever tasted."

"Why haven't you suggested we eat here before now?" he asked. He often talked restaurants with his sister. She loved Italian but he could remember her mentioning this place only once before.

She hesitated. "It was Jack's and my favorite spot. Mostly I didn't want to bring up a bunch of hurtful memories so I've avoided coming here ever since our breakup, which is silly."

Aren hesitated. "Aren't you afraid of running into Jack?"

Josie shook her head. "He probably doesn't want

to chance meeting up with me in the place we used to think of as 'our restaurant.' "

Aren hoped his sister was right. Then, on second thought, it might serve Jack and Josie well if they did happen to stumble across each other. If Jack's reaction was even close to his sister's, then perhaps there was hope for the two of them. And if matters could be patched up between the pair, just maybe it could happen for him and Lucie. Aren frowned. His mind was playing silly tricks on him.

Aren held the door open for his sister. She paused just inside the restaurant and whispered, "And if Jack does happen to show I'll smile and pretend I'm having the time of my life."

"Right," Aren whispered back.

The hostess smiled warmly when she saw Josie.

"Oh, Miss, it's so good to see you."

"You, too," Josie said. "Is my favorite table available?"

Aren didn't pay much attention to the exchange between the two women as he was distracted by the enticing scents coming from the kitchen. He momentarily closed his eyes and breathed in deeply. A mixture of garlic and spices, tomatoes and basil. If the aroma was anything to go by he was in for a treat.

In just a matter of minutes they were escorted to a table and handed menus. Even before Aren had a chance to review the selections, breadsticks were delivered to their table.

"The breadsticks are baked here every afternoon," Josie told him. "They're divine. Jack always said we could make a meal out of them alone."

"How's the ravioli?" he asked, more interested in studying the menu. He had to admit he was impressed.

A pained look bled into Josie's expression. "The cheese ravioli were Jack's favorite. He'd order them every time we dined here, and we came at least once a week."

"What about you? What did you order?"

She smiled then. "Everything. The food is so good, I wanted to try every last thing on the menu. I'd worked my way through the appetizers and the salads and I was halfway through the entrées when we split."

"Did you have a favorite?"

"That's just it. Every dish is simply wonderful. I was even inspired to try to make some of the appetizers myself, especially the rolled eggplant, but my attempts were never as good as what we had here, so we just kept coming back week after week."

The waiter came for their order and Aren asked for the cheese-stuffed ravioli. Josie had just finished telling the waiter she wanted to try their seafood spaghetti when she abruptly went still. Aren didn't need anyone to tell him Josie had spied Jack. He could almost have guaranteed this would happen.

Leaning across the table, Aren asked, "Is Miss Universe with him?"

Josie held her head high and nodded ever so slightly. "Oh, yes, and she's as gorgeous as ever."

Because Aren's back was to the entrance, he couldn't see, and turning around to look would have upset Josie, although he was tempted.

Josie smiled and nodded. "He just saw me," she said under her breath.

"And?"

"And he looks pretty shaken up. Good. Now he knows how I felt when I saw him last Saturday night." She leaned across the table and whispered, "Laugh."

Aren blinked. "I beg your pardon?"

"Don't be dense. I want you to laugh as if I'm the funniest, most clever woman you've ever met in your life."

"Josie." Aren wasn't up to playing games.

"Please, Aren, do this for me. I'll never ask anything of you again as long as I live."

That was a likely story. He was beginning to think his sister had set up this entire meeting and he'd blindly walked into her plans.

"Please." Her eyes pleaded with him.

"All right, all right." He chuckled and managed a weak smile.

"Louder," Josie whispered.

"This is ridiculous." He should have suspected something was up when Josie mentioned a favorite table and insisted on sitting facing the door.

To keep the peace, Aren laughed again, with a bit more energy this time.

She smiled with a dreamy expression. "That was perfect."

"Thanks."

Josie leaned closer and became more animated, laughing softly while Aren did his best not to roll his eyes. His sister was overdoing it. She pressed her hand over her heart and smiled at him as though she hung on every little word Aren uttered.

"The least you could do is play along," his sister hissed when he glared back at her.

"What's Jack doing now?" Aren asked.

Josie looked mighty pleased with herself. "He hasn't been able to take his eyes off us."

"Where's he sitting?"

"Two tables over against the wall."

Aren set his napkin on the tabletop, then he stood up without a word.

"What are you doing?" Josie whispered as a worried look came over her features. "Aren, if you do what I think you're about to do, I swear I'll never speak to you again."

He grinned and shrugged. "I should be so lucky."

"Aren," she pleaded frantically, half-standing as though to stop him.

He had no intention of being dissuaded. His sister was miserable and if Jack hadn't been able to take his eyes off her then Aren suspected Jack felt the same way about her.

Turning away from his sister, Aren crossed the short distance between the two tables. As Aren approached, Jack set aside his napkin and stood. He was a good three inches taller than Aren and outweighed him by twenty pounds, but Aren wasn't looking to best the other man.

"You must be Jack," he said and extended his hand. "Aren Fairchild, Josie's brother."

The other man broke into an instant smile.

Aren dared not look in Josie's direction. "It seems you and my sister have had a misunderstanding."

"Excuse me." The woman with Jack didn't look the least bit pleased. "I'm not invisible, you know."

Jack appeared to have completely forgotten the other woman. "Oh, sorry. Pamela, this is the brother of the woman I mentioned earlier."

"You mean the one you seem to drag into every conversation?"

Jack looked away and didn't answer.

"It seems I ordered your favorite meal. It's about to be delivered. Why don't you join my sister and I'll introduce myself to Pamela."

"Now just a minute. Don't I have a say in this?" Jack's date demanded.

"Apparently not," Aren answered. Jack was already halfway across the restaurant.

Aren pulled out the chair and sat down with Pamela. She was pretty enough, he supposed, but two minutes in her company and it was clear she was high maintenance. After a good ten minutes she scooted out of her chair and said, "Tell Jack it would be best if he not contact me again."

Aren waved her off. "It might be best if you tell him that yourself."

"Then I will. Gladly."

Sure enough Pamela pranced across the room to the table where Jack sat with Josie. Their heads were together and whatever their problem had been, it wasn't in evidence now.

Jack stood as Pamela approached. Aren wasn't privy to whatever the other woman had to say but apparently she wanted nothing more to do with him. She left in a huff.

Seeing that he'd accomplished his mission, Aren left a generous tip on the table before getting up to leave. He felt more than conspicuous as every eye in the restaurant was on him. He could only imagine that speculation among the diners must be rampant. On his way out the door, Josie caught his eye and blew him a kiss. He returned it with a wave and was off.

His apartment felt cold and dark when he let himself in. He felt good about helping his sister and Jack. He hoped it had just been prewedding jitters that had set them off course. Seeing them together this evening made it clear neither one was happy apart. He hoped they would be able to settle the matter once and for all.

His phone rang close to midnight, waking Aren out of a sound sleep.

"Thank you," Josie whispered.

"You're welcome. Can I go back to sleep now?"

"No. Do you want to come over so we can talk?"

"Josie, I'm in bed."

"Okay, be a party pooper, see if I care."

"I'm happy for you." And he was, but at the moment he was too tired and he wanted to get back to his dream . . . a dream that involved Lucie.

Chapter Sixteen

It was Christmas Eve and Lucie should be excited and happy. She wasn't. Instead her heart was heavy. It'd been that way from the moment she had last talked to Aren. He hadn't contacted her and pride wouldn't allow her to reach out to him. She faithfully read his column and noticed that he wasn't quite as cutting as he had been, at least in her mind. She hungered for news from him but none came.

Her mother walked into the kitchen where Lucie sat with her morning cup of coffee. Sammy rested by her feet. "Come on, sweetie, smile," Wendy urged. "It's Christmas Eve." Her mother's happiness brightened the room.

"I am smiling, Mom. I'm grateful for this time off." They'd decided to close the restaurant for the next two days and Lucie welcomed the break. She hadn't been in the Christmas spirit much and had put off shopping and wrapping until the last minute.

Wendy reached for the coffeepot and poured her own mug and then sat down and tested her blood sugar. Without a word, she stood and brought out a container of orange juice. "Are you going to contact Aren?" she asked as if it were a little thing.

"No."

Her mother's shoulders sagged with disappointment. "Why not?"

"Mom, we've been through this a dozen times. It's over between us."

"And that's what you want?" Her mother's skeptical look said it all.

Lucie didn't answer because she longed for Aren, she missed him and wished with every part of her being that things could be different. But he was who he was and she couldn't change that.

"I thought I'd go into the city this morning," Lucie announced, doing her best to sound excited and upbeat. "I have some shopping left and I need to run a couple of other errands, too."

"Don't be late for dinner," Wendy told her after Lucie reached for her coat and purse.

"I won't."

Actually what Lucie wanted most was to escape and forget this was Christmas Eve. What had happened between her and Aren remained fresh in her mind. If she kept herself busy, she might be distracted enough to put Aren out of her thoughts and be able to appreciate the season at least a little bit. That was her hope. A day in the city was bound to help.

———

"Do you see how miserable Lucie is?" Will asked Mercy.

"I couldn't help but notice." Mercy and her two friends stayed close to their young charge as Will followed Lucie onto the subway leading into Manhattan.

Will had been a fast learner, although he was still tempted to intervene in the lives of humans. Mercy recognized that he'd picked up the habit from the three of them. They really did try to walk the straight-and-narrow path, and somehow, to this point, they'd been able to answer the prayers as God intended even if the path made several sharp twists every now and again.

Once the subway arrived at her stop, Lucie walked up the steps to the Manhattan sidewalk. The city was crazy busy with shoppers darting from store to store. Everyone seemed to be in a terrible rush.

"Is it always like this on Christmas Eve?" Will asked, darting around the bustling crowds and doing his best to stay out of their way.

"Always," Shirley insisted. "Sometimes it's even worse."

"Busier than this?" Will appeared to find that hard to believe.

"Oh, yes, I remember the year—"

"Where's Lucie going now?" Will interrupted.

Mercy knew he felt responsible for the mix-up in timing for Lucie and Aren to meet and wanted more than anything to make matters right. She couldn't allow Will to intervene, though. Gabriel had been quite specific. Lucie and Aren had to work this out themselves, which made a reconciliation all the more difficult. Both were prideful and stubborn.

"Is she really going to ignore Aren over Christmas?" Will demanded.

"She's ignored him to this point," Goodness reminded them.

"She didn't even send him a Christmas card."

"Nothing," Mercy confirmed.

"Did Aren send her a card?" Shirley asked. "It wouldn't have hurt him any to make an effort."

"I agree, he should have done something," Will said. "Don't you just want to shake these humans? They're impossible."

"My dear young charge, you have only seen the tip of the iceberg when it comes to dealing with humans."

"The what?"

"Never mind." Goodness patted Will's upper arm. "One day we'll show you the Arctic."

"Is that close to New York?"

"It's a bit farther north," Mercy explained.

"Are humans there as stubborn as they are here?"

"Oh, yes, humans are the same everywhere."

"Amazing. And God still loves them?"

"It's hard to comprehend, but He does. It's really incredible when you think about how slow-witted they are."

"Where's Lucie headed now?" Will asked, frantically following her into a store.

"Oh, this is one of my favorite spots in the whole world."

"What is it?" Will cried, jumping on the escalator behind Lucie.

"It's a bookstore," Mercy answered and grabbed Shirley by the belt in order to keep her away from the children's section.

Shirley sighed with disappointment. "I wasn't going to get into any trouble."

"Maybe so, but I'm playing it safe just in case."

"What is Lucie looking for?" Will asked, staying close on the chef's heels.

"I imagine she's searching for a special book to give as a present," Goodness supplied. "This is a bookstore, you realize."

"A very big one with lots of people." Shirley darted out of the way.

"Look, Lucie found a quiet corner and is sitting down."

"I'll join her," Shirley insisted. "Running around like this is wearing me out."

"I think we're all a little frazzled."

"You are all working overly hard, don't you think?"

At the sound of Gabriel's booming voice the four

angels jumped and whirled around. "And in addition you're looking guilty." His voice rumbled so much it was a wonder the walls didn't tremble. "Is there something the four of you wish to tell me?"

Will, acting braver than Mercy had ever seen him, stepped forward. "We need to do something and fast."

"You mean you want to intervene?"

"Yes, I feel responsible for Lucie and Aren. I introduced them when they weren't scheduled to meet and now everything has gone awry and they're separated and miserable."

Gabriel sadly shook his head. "It's not up to us. The lesson both Aren and Lucie need to learn is about pride and stubbornness. If they can't resolve this minor life issue then their relationship is already doomed. Love is about acceptance and generosity of spirit, and frankly I don't see that in either of them."

"I do," Will challenged. "Look at what Lucie and her mother did for the homeless."

"And look at how willing Aren was to pitch in and help," Goodness added.

"He was wonderful with the children," Shirley reminded Gabriel.

"Yes, now that you mention it, he was."

"See, there is hope for Lucie and Aren," Will insisted. "If only you'd allow us to—"

"No." Gabriel raised his finger, stopping Will

from speaking further. "Intervention is out of the question."

He left them then and Mercy watched as young Will's shoulders sagged with disappointment. Glancing over her shoulder, Mercy lowered her voice. "I don't mean to cause problems, but I think I might have an idea."

"Does it involve Lucie and Aren?" Will asked with hopeful expectation.

She cocked her head to one side and lowered her voice. "Indirectly."

Goodness perked up right away. "Now, this sounds promising."

"Who does it involve, then?" Shirley remained the skeptic.

"You'll see," she said. "Follow me."

"Should I leave Lucie?" Will asked, and seemed doubtful.

"She'll be fine, trust me."

Will complied, although reluctantly.

"I just hope we're doing the right thing," Shirley said, the last to turn away from Lucie. "I've gotten into a heap of trouble before listening to Mercy."

"I have a good feeling about this," Goodness added. "Mercy's got great ideas."

Lucie's cellphone beeped, indicating she had a text message. She reached in the side pocket of her purse and grabbed her phone. The number was one she didn't recognize. With a tap of her finger she read the message. Four o'clock on top of the Empire State Building.

Frowning, Lucie tucked her cell back inside her purse while she mulled over who could possibly have sent her the text. Her first thought was that it might be Aren. It wasn't though. She would have recognized his cell number.

Well, she wasn't going. It would be ridiculous. She had several errands yet to run. Later she had dinner plans with her mother, and then that evening the two of them would attend Christmas Eve services at their church. Lucie had everything all planned out. Her day didn't leave time for a wild-goose chase to the Empire State Building.

She wasn't doing it.

Ten minutes later she glanced at her watch. Three thirty-three.

Even if she wanted to she would never reach the Empire State Building in time, and getting a cab in the city at this time of day and on Christmas Eve would be next to impossible.

No sooner had the thought entered her mind than a taxi pulled up to the curb next to her. A woman climbed out.

Lucie stared in amazement as no one rushed to get inside.

"You coming or not, lady?" the cabbie demanded. "I got people waiting."

Looking around, Lucie slapped her hand against her chest. "Are you talking to me?"

"You waved me down, didn't you?"

"Ah . . . no."

"Fine, then."

He started to pull away but Lucie stopped him. Running a couple of steps, she caught up with him and opened the passenger door. "Can you get me to the Empire State Building before four o'clock?"

"In this traffic? You're joking, right?"

"Do what you can." Lucie hadn't intended to follow the instructions from her text and at the same time she couldn't stop herself. Even if Aren hadn't sent the message, she needed to know who had and why.

The taxi driver eased back into the bumper-to-bumper traffic. "It'll be a miracle if we make your four o'clock appointment."

"Do your best . . . if I don't make it, then I don't make it." Even now Lucie wasn't sure why she was in the cab. This was someone's idea of a joke and a bad one at that. Perhaps Aren was behind it, luring her to this destination point to keep her waiting, the way she had kept him waiting last January.

Even while the thought raced through her mind, she knew he would never do that. It wasn't in his nature to pull something that twisted.

Perhaps it was hope that convinced her to make her way there. A mixed-up kind of hope that led her to believe that somehow she and Aren could work things out.

"Well, would you look at that?" the cabbie whispered under his breath.

"I'm sorry?" Lucie said, leaning forward. Because she'd been wrapped up in her own thoughts she hadn't heard the driver.

"Fifth Avenue," he said and gestured for her to look out the windshield.

Lucie looked but didn't see anything. "What about it?"

"It's clear. It's like the parting of the Red Sea. I've got an entire lane to myself. I've been driving a cab for nearly twenty years and I've never seen anything like this happen. You'd think I had a police escort."

"Oh?" Lucie wasn't sure what to say.

"You got an angel on your shoulder or something?" he called back to Lucie.

"No . . . I don't think so." Lucie was beginning to think she had some kind of crazy karma when it came to cabs. Her last experience had been equally unexplainable, with the newspaper flying around and the windows moving up and down of their own accord. Now this. She watched as the traffic seemed to divide just for them.

In no time at all the cab pulled to the curb outside the iconic skyscraper. The driver scratched the side of his head and seemed utterly amazed. "I don't believe this but it's five minutes to four. We made it all the way downtown in heavy traffic in unbelievable time. I'd say it's a Christmas miracle, but I'm not saying a word to anyone—who'd believe me?"

"Five minutes early," Lucie repeated in a state of shock herself.

She paid the driver and climbed out of the cab. Standing on the street, she held on to her knitted hat and looked up at the skyscraper.

Now that she was here, she might as well find out what this cryptic message was all about. The line to pay for the elevator ride and the view on the 102nd floor moved quickly. The woman selling tickets glanced at her watch. "We're closing at four today, seeing that it's Christmas Eve."

"I can promise you that I won't be long."

The woman handed Lucie her ticket and she moved with the others waiting for what must be the last ride of the day up the elevator. She'd been to the top floor once before, but that had been years ago. If Lucie remembered, she'd been on a field trip with her fifth-grade class. Although she was young, she'd been impressed with the story of the structure, which first opened in 1931, just after the start of the Great Depression.

As she stepped out of the elevator, Lucie immediately went outside. The lights of the city had started to turn on and she stood mesmerized by the incredible three-hundred-sixty-degree view. Although she'd promised the woman selling the tickets she wouldn't be long, Lucie felt drawn to the view. The sadness that had enveloped her since her last conversation with Aren lifted. All at once she knew what she had to do.

She needed to phone Aren. When they last spoke she claimed she needed a breather. Well, she'd had one.

Digging into her purse, she reached for her phone and scrolled through her contacts until she found his name. A smile lit up her face as she initiated the call.

It rang four times and then went to voice mail.

Chapter Seventeen

What surprised Aren the most was how many people had found their way to the top of the Empire State Building on Christmas Eve. Although it was closing time and the guards were anxiously glancing at their watches, no one seemed to be in a hurry to leave. Especially him.

Earlier in the day Aren had gotten a text from Jack asking to meet him there at four, but Jack was nowhere to be found.

It didn't take Aren long to figure out the reason behind Jack's request. He strongly suspected that the other man was about to give Josie back the engagement ring she'd returned. Aren couldn't be happier for his sister.

Glancing at his watch, he scanned the area and shrugged. One of the guards announced the deck had to be cleared within the next fifteen minutes. The crowd started to thin out as several people headed toward the elevator. It would be just like his sister to be late to her own engagement. Funny though, both Jack and Josie were late.

Something unavoidable must have come up. Aren reached for his phone to call Jack and find out what was up. To his surprise he discovered that he'd inadvertently turned off the ringer and had missed a number of calls. As he was scanning the numbers, preoccupied with the task at hand, he bumped into someone behind him.

"Excuse me," he said, turning to apologize. The words froze on his lips. "Lucie?"

"Aren?"

"What are you doing here?" he asked, his mind spinning.

"I got a text . . ."

She got a text? "So did I."

"I didn't recognize the phone number . . . I wasn't going to come but then I found myself in a taxi and the driver said it would be impossible to get here before four but we did and he said it was a Christmas miracle, like the parting of the Red Sea, which I don't think happened in December, but then I don't know for sure." She stopped abruptly as she realized she was jabbering. "Oh, Aren, Aren, I'm so happy to see you." With that she threw her arms around his neck.

Caught off guard, Aren stumbled two steps back. He didn't know what had happened or how they both happened to be at the same place at the same time, but he was in no mood to question it. He was simply too pleased to care. Looping his arms around her waist, Aren closed his eyes and held Lucie close to his heart.

She said she'd received a Christmas miracle with some crazy taxi ride. Well, he'd gotten one of his own and that was Lucie clinging to him and chattering away so fast he could barely understand a word she said.

"I was being silly and foolish and—"

Aren eased her away and silenced her by placing his finger against her lips. Immediately she stopped talking and blinked several times. Smiling down at her, Aren brushed the hair from her face.

"We were both being silly and foolish," he said.

"My life is crazy . . . the restaurant means everything. It has to succeed, but I can't walk away from you. I just can't."

"Good." He kissed her then and it felt as if it'd been months since he'd experienced anything even close to the contentment he found with Lucie in his arms. "I can't walk away from you either."

"I tried to call you."

"When?"

"Just now and it went to voice mail and I thought . . . I assumed you didn't want to talk to me and I thought I'd ruined everything."

"My ringer got turned off. I don't remember doing that, but apparently I did."

"Who sent you the text, because I don't know who it was that sent mine?" she asked, looking up at him, her eyes bright with happiness.

"Jack."

"Who's Jack?"

"Josie's soon-to-be husband. They just recently got back together. I assumed he was going to propose to my sister a second time."

"A second time?"

"Don't ask, it's a long story."

Lucie reached for her cell in the side pocket outside her purse and showed Aren her text. "Is this Jack's number?"

Aren looked at it and frowned. "No. That number belongs to my sister."

"How did Josie get my cell number?"

"I have no idea." For Josie to have the contact information for Lucie was as much a mystery to Aren as it was to Lucie. "What I can tell you is fairly obvious. My sister and Jack teamed up to bring us back together."

"It worked. Oh, Aren, Merry Christmas."

"Merry Christmas, my love."

"Your love. You mean you're willing to give us another chance?"

"Definitely."

Lucie blinked back tears. "I swear, this is the best Christmas of my life."

"Mine, too." Closing his eyes, he kissed her forehead. "The last time I was here I waited, hoping with all my heart that you'd show. This time I had no expectation of seeing you and here you are."

"I'm so glad I'm here . . . and even happier that you are, too."

"Good."

Then, as if it suddenly dawned on her, she said, "You'll come home with me, won't you? Mom will be ecstatic to see you. She's got the most wonderful dinner planned. It's far more than the two of us could ever eat, so please say you'll join us and then later there's church. The music is just beautiful and I can't think of a better person to spend Christmas Eve with than you."

Aren couldn't think of a better way either.

"You'll have dinner with us, won't you?" Her eyes widened as she pleaded with him.

Aren nodded.

Lucie hugged him tight. "I've been so miserable and too stubborn to admit it. I've learned so much about myself. Aren, oh, Aren, I've been such an idiot."

"I have been, too."

"No," she argued, intent on accepting the blame. "You were more than reasonable and I was—"

He stopped her the only way he could think of and that was by taking her in his arms and kissing her senseless until they were interrupted by the guard.

"Hey, folks, I hate to interrupt a romantic moment, but we're closing down for the night."

"Oh, sorry," Lucie whispered.

Aren wrapped his arm around her waist. Holding on to each other they took the express elevator down to the ground floor. As soon as they were outside Aren reached for his cell.

"Who are you calling?" Lucie asked.

"My sister, seeing that she arranged all this." He tapped his contact list and scrolled down to her name. It rang three times before she answered.

"This better be important," Josie whispered. "Jack's here and he just gave me my engagement ring back."

"I wanted to thank you, actually both Lucie and I send our appreciation."

"Ah . . . for what?"

"The text you sent her and the one Jack sent me."

"What text?"

"Come on, Josie, the jig is up. Lucie got your text and I got the one Jack sent. The two of us met up at the Empire State Building just the way you planned."

"Hold on, bro. I didn't send Lucie any text."

"You didn't?" This wasn't making any sense. "Check your phone, will you?"

"Sure, but it won't do any good. I know what I sent and it wasn't anything about the Empire State Building, and for that matter how would I get Lucie's cell number?"

Good question, and one Aren had already considered. "Okay," he said, "I guess there's been more than one Christmas miracle. Congratulations to you and Jack. I'm heading over to Lucie's for dinner and church, but will connect with you in the morning."

"Merry Christmas, Aren."

"Merry Christmas." His sister sounded like the happiest woman in the world. He understood because he was walking on cloud nine himself.

"Do you want to explain how Josie got Lucie's cell number?" Gabriel asked Mercy and her friends. They'd gathered in the choir loft of the Brooklyn church for the Christmas Eve services. Aren, Lucie, and Wendy sat in the pew midway up on the left-hand side.

Aren and Lucie shared a hymnal. Their voices blended beautifully as they sang the classic Christmas carol "Silent Night." Unfortunately they had yet to hear the angel choir, which was beyond anything on earth, but thankfully they would one day.

"Ah . . ."

"Mercy, why do I think this is your doing?" Gabriel pressed.

"We had to do something," Will explained. "I felt personally responsible for this mess, so we tweaked a few of your instructions and made it work."

"What's going to happen with them?" Goodness pried. "You know the future. We don't."

"You answer my question first," Gabriel demanded.

"Well, you said we couldn't interfere in their

lives," Will said, although a reminder wasn't necessary.

"Interfere in their lives *again*," Gabriel corrected.

"Right," Will added.

"And so . . ." Gabriel fixed his gaze on Mercy.

"Why are you staring at me?" she asked, doing her utmost to look as innocent as a budding rose.

"Because you have always been the ringleader when it came to mischief."

"Me?" Mercy was downright offended. Of the four of them she was the one who kept everyone in check. "That is grossly unfair," she protested. "I have prevented more interferences on Earth than you will ever know about."

"She has," Goodness said, coming to Mercy's defense.

"Mercy has done her best to keep us in line."

Gabriel frowned. "Apparently with little success."

Mercy's wings sank all the way to the floor. "Should . . . do you want me to . . ."

"Mercy, no," Goodness cried and came to stand at her friend's side.

"If anyone should go, it'll be me," Shirley insisted, coming to stand on the other side of Mercy.

"Or me," Will chimed in. "I can probably get a transfer."

Gabriel held up his hand, putting an end to their chatter. "In light of the season I think we might be able to overlook certain transgressions."

"We could?" Mercy asked with a heart filled with hope. Apparently Gabriel was in a generous mood.

"It isn't like you did anything outrageous, like kidnap a camel and lead it outside a theater? That would be incomprehensible."

Goodness sucked in her breath and held it so long she was in danger of turning blue. Mercy slapped her friend's back and Goodness exhaled so loudly the pipe organ let out a B flat all on its own. Several people in the congregation turned toward the choir loft.

"It could have been worse. Right?" Gabriel asked, tapping his toe impatiently.

The four all stared down at their feet as if searching for a lost button, looking in every direction except at Gabriel.

"Right?" Gabriel asked again.

"Right," Mercy answered weakly.

"One of you might have done something really crazy, like interrupt a Broadway play and suspend the actors in the air without any visible means of support."

Mercy swallowed uncomfortably.

"We'd never do anything like that," Goodness muttered.

"Or play a tuba."

"I didn't play the tuba," Will insisted. "I just looked at it." Then realizing what he'd said, he slapped his hand over his mouth.

"Well, my friends," Gabriel said, smiling now.

"Despite everything, you managed to answer Wendy's prayer. Lucie and Aren are together and they were able to meet at the Empire State Building."

"Does their relationship last?" Will asked.

Gabriel nodded. "Yes. They will be married in October next year."

"Oh good."

"Children?"

"Two. A boy and a girl."

"What about the restaurant?"

"What about Aren? Will he continue to write for the newspaper?"

"One question at a time, my friends," Gabriel said, leaning over the choir railing to look down upon Aren and Lucie. He smiled and then turned to look at the four Prayer Ambassadors. "The restaurant will do exceptionally well and Wendy's investment will pay rich dividends. The two will sell Heavenly Delights for twice what they put into it in five years' time, after Lucie delivers her daughter."

"That's wonderful, but what will Lucie do without the restaurant? She loves to cook."

"She won't abandon her career entirely. She's going to become a recipe developer for some of the better-known celebrity chefs across America. It's the perfect job for her as she'll be able to stay home with the children."

"What about Aren?"

"Now, that's a bit of a surprise."

"How so?" Goodness asked.

"Aren will leave the newspaper shortly after he sells his first novel."

"Aren writes fiction?"

"It's a secret passion he has. He's been working on this book in his spare time for several years and when it sells, it will be an instant success beyond anything he or Lucie could imagine."

"Does he get a movie deal?" Goodness asked. "Oh, Gabriel, can we be in it? Can we, oh, can we?"

The look Gabriel cast her was all the answer they needed.

"This is just wonderful." Mercy rubbed her palms together with delight. It was even better than she'd imagined.

"They will have a good life together, and so will Josie and Jack." Gabriel spread his massive wings over the four. "Are you ready to head back to heaven?" he asked.

"We are," Mercy said, answering for them all.

And so they returned to the realms of glory. As they drew near, Mercy could hear the strains of music unlike anything ever heard on Earth. The celebration of the infant born in a stable over two thousand years earlier was just getting started.

PEPPERMINT BARK

8 medium-sized candy canes

12 oz (about 2 cups) good quality semisweet chocolate (bars or chips)

12 oz (about 2 cups) white chocolate (bars or chips). Choose the ones made with cocoa butter.

Finely crush the candy canes, using a plastic bag and rolling pin or a food processor.

Cover a cookie sheet with aluminum foil. Gently melt the semisweet chocolate in a double boiler or in a bowl in the microwave on 50 percent power. Begin with 1 minute at 50 percent power, stir, and follow by repeat cycles of 30 seconds at 50 percent power—stirring between cycles—as often as needed until melted and smooth. Gentle melting prevents burning and helps preserve the tempering of the chocolate.

Pour the melted semisweet chocolate onto the aluminum foil and spread it to a size of about 8" x 10".

The sizing isn't etched in stone. You can make the bark thicker or thinner, depending on what you prefer. Refrigerate the semisweet chocolate layer while you're preparing the white chocolate/peppermint layer.

Melt the white chocolate using the same melting method as for the semisweet. Once it's melted, stir in about ¾ of the crushed peppermint candy. Set the mixture aside at room temperature (to cool a little) until the semisweet layer is ready. The chocolate should still be a *little* soft, a little sticky, but *not at all* liquid.

Pour the white chocolate onto the semisweet chocolate layer and gently spread it evenly toward the edges. Sprinkle the remainder of the crushed peppermint on top, then refrigerate until the chocolate is hardened. You can then break it by hand, or score it and break it.

The peppermint bark refrigerates well, freezes well, ships well, and tastes quite wonderful at room temperature . . . ideally with a cup of coffee or tea and a good book.

If *Angels at the Table* warmed your heart,
you won't want to miss Debbie Macomber's
next delightful Christmas tale

Starry Night

Read on for a sneak peek at the holiday story
that Debbie Macomber is calling
one of the most romantic books
she's ever written.

Available now from Ballantine Books

Chapter One

Carrie Slayton's feet were killing her. She'd spent the last ninety minutes standing in two-inch heels at a charity art auction in a swanky studio in downtown Chicago. She couldn't understand how shoes that matched her black dress so beautifully could be this painful. Vanity, thy name is fashion.

"My name is spelled with two *l*'s," the middle-aged woman, dripping in diamonds, reminded her. "That's Michelle, with two *l*'s."

"Got it." Carrie underlined the correct spelling. Michelle, spelled with two *l*'s, had just spent thirty thousand dollars for the most ridiculous piece of art Carrie had ever seen. True, it was for a good cause, but now she seemed to feel her name needed to be mentioned in the news article Carrie would write for the next edition of the *Chicago Herald*.

"It would be wonderful to have my husband's and my picture to go along with your article," Michelle added. "Perhaps you should take it in front of the painting."

Carrie looked over her shoulder at Harry, the

photographer who'd accompanied her from the newspaper.

"Of course, Lloyd and I would want approval of any photograph you choose to publish."

"Of course," Carrie said, doing her best to keep a smile in place. If she didn't get out of these shoes soon, her feet would be permanently deformed. She wiggled her toes, hoping for relief. Instead they ached even worse.

Harry, bless his heart, dutifully stepped forward, camera in hand, and flashed two or three photos of the couple posing in front of what might have been a red flower or a painting of a squished tomato or possibly the aftermath of a murder scene. Carrie had yet to decide which. The title of the work didn't offer a clue. *Red*. Yes, the painting was in that color, but exactly what it depicted remained a mystery.

"Isn't it stunning?" Michelle asked when she noticed Carrie staring at the canvas.

Carrie tilted her head one way and then another, looking for some clue as to its possible significance. Then, noticing that Michelle, spelled with two *l*'s, was waiting for her response, she said, "Oh yes, it's amazing."

Harry didn't bother to hide his smile, knowing that all Carrie really wanted was to get out of those ridiculous shoes. And to think she'd gotten her journalism degree for this!

Carrie knew she was fortunate to have a job with such a prestigious newspaper. A professor had pulled in a favor and gotten her the interview. Carrie had been stunned when she'd been hired. Surprised and overjoyed.

Two years later, she was less so. Her assignment was the society page. When she was hired, she'd been told that eventually she'd be able to write meatier pieces, do interviews and human-interest stories. To this point, it hadn't happened. Carrie felt trapped, frustrated, and underappreciated. She felt her talent was being wasted.

To make matters worse, her entire family lived in the Pacific Northwest. Carrie had left everything she knew and loved behind, including Steve, her college sweetheart. He'd married less than six months after she took the position in Chicago. It hadn't taken him long, she noted. The worst part was that Carrie was far too busy reporting on social events to have time for much of a social life herself. She dated occasionally, but she hadn't found anyone who made her heart race. Dave Schneider, the man she'd been seeing most recently, was more of a friend than a love interest. She supposed after Steve she was a bit hesitant to get involved again. Maybe once she left the *Herald* and moved home to write for a newspaper in the Seattle area, like she planned, things would be different.

Back inside her condo, Carrie gingerly removed her shoes and sighed with relief.

This was it. She was done. First thing in the morning she would hand in her two-week notice, sublet her condo, and take her chances in the job market in Seattle. If the managing editor, Nash Jorgen, refused to give her the opportunity to prove she had what it took, then why stay? She refused to be pigeonholed.

That decided, Carrie limped into her bedroom and fell into bed, tired, frustrated, and determined to make a change.

"You can't be serious," argued Sophie Peterson, her closest friend at the newspaper, when Carrie told her of her decision.

"I'm totally serious," she said as she hobbled to her desk.

"What's wrong with your foot?" Sophie asked, tagging behind her.

"Stupidity. This gorgeous pair of shoes was only available in a half-size smaller than what I normally wear. They were so perfect, and they were buy one pair, get the second half off. I couldn't resist, but now I'm paying for it."

"Carrie, don't do it."

"Don't worry, I have no intention of wearing those heels again. I tossed them in a bag for charity."

"Not that," Sophie argued. "Don't hand in your notice! You're needed here."

"Not as a reporter," Carrie assured her, dumping

her purse in her bottom drawer and shucking off her thick winter coat. "Sorry, my mind is made up. You and I both know Nash will never give me a decent assignment."

"You're your own worst enemy." Sophie leaned against the wall that separated their two cubicles and crossed her arms and ankles.

"How's that?"

"Well, for one thing, you're the perfect fit for the society page. You're drop-dead gorgeous, tall and thin. It doesn't hurt that you look fabulous in a slinky black dress and a pair of spike heels. Even if I could get my hair to grow that thick, long, and curly without perming the living daylights out of it, Nash would never consider someone like me. It isn't any wonder he wants you on the job. Give the guy a little credit, will you? He knows what he's doing."

"If looks are the only criteria—"

"There's more," Sophie said, cutting her off. "You're great with people. All you need to do is bat those baby blues at them and strangers open up to you. It's a gift, I tell you, a real gift."

"Okay, I'm friendly, but this isn't the kind of writing I want to do. I've got my heart set on being a reporter, a real reporter, writing about real news and interesting people." In the beginning, Carrie had been flattered by the way people went out of their way to introduce themselves at the events she covered. It didn't take long for her to recognize that they were looking for her to mention their names in print. What shocked her was the extent people were willing to go in order to be noticed. She was quickly becoming jaded, and this bothered her even more than Nash's lack of faith in her abilities.

The holidays were the worst, and while it was only early November, the frenzy had already started. The list of parties Nash assigned her to attend was already mammoth. Halloween decorations were still arranged around her desk, and already there was a Christmas tree in the display window of the department store across the street.

Determined to stick with her plan, Carrie went directly into Nash Jorgen's office.

A veteran newsman, Nash glanced up from his computer screen and glared in her direction. He seemed to sense this wasn't a social visit. His shoulders rose with a weary sigh. "What now?" he growled.

"I'm handing in my two-week notice." If she'd been looking for a response, she would have been disappointed.

He blinked a couple of times, ran his hand down the side of his day-old beard, and asked, "Any particular reason?"

"I hoped to prove I can be a darn good reporter, but I'll never get a chance writing anything more than copy for society weddings. You said when you hired me that you'd give me a shot at reporting real news."

"I don't remember what I said. What's wrong with what you're writing now? You're good."

"It isn't what I want to write."

"So? You make the best of it, pay your dues, and in time you'll get the break you're looking for."

Carrie was tired of waiting. She straightened her shoulders, her resolve tightening. "I know I'm fortunate to work for the *Herald*. It was a real coup to get this position, but this isn't the career I wanted. You give me no choice." She set her letter of resignation on his desk.

This got Nash's attention. He swiveled his chair around to look at her once more. His frown darkened, and he ran his hand through his thinning hair. "You really are serious, aren't you?"

A chill went down her spine. Nash was actually listening. "Yes, I'm serious."

"Fine, then." He reached across his desk and picked up a hardcover book and handed it to her. "Find Finn Dalton, get an interview, and write me a story I can print."

She grabbed hold of the book, not recognizing the author's name. "And if I do?"

"Well, first, there's a snowball's chance of you even locating him. Every reporter in the universe is dying to interview him. But if you get lucky and he's willing to talk and we print the piece, then I'll take you off the society page."

Carrie wavered. He seemed to be offering her a chance, as impossible as it might seem. Now it was up to her to prove herself. She dared not show him how excited she was. "I'll find him."

He snickered as though he found her confidence amusing, and then sobered. He regarded her with the same dark frown he had earlier before a slow, easy smile slid over his harsh features. "I bet you will. Now, listen up—if you get an interview with Finn Dalton, you can have any assignment you want."

Taking small steps, Carrie backed out of the office. She pointed at Nash. "I'm holding you to your word."

The managing editor was already back to reading his computer screen and didn't appear to have heard her. It didn't matter; she'd heard him, and he'd come across loud and clear.

Once she was out of his office, she examined the book to see the author photo, but couldn't find one, not even on the inside back flap.

Walking back to her cubicle, she paused at Sophie's instead. "You ever heard of Finn Dalton?"

Sophie's eyebrows lifted on her round face. "You mean you haven't?"

"No." The book title wasn't much help. *Alone.* That told her next to nothing. The jacket revealed a snow-covered landscape with a scattering of stubby trees.

Sophie shook her head. "Have you been living under a rock?"

"No. Who is this guy?"

"He's a survivalist who lives alone someplace in the Alaskan wilderness."

"Oh." That was a bit daunting, but Carrie considered herself up to the challenge. She'd been born and raised in Washington state. She'd hoped to join her family for Thanksgiving, but if she needed to use her vacation time to find Finn Dalton, then she was willing to.

"His book has been on the best-seller lists for nearly seven months, mostly at the number-one position."

Carrie was impressed. "What does he write about?"

"He's the kind of guy you can set loose in the wild with a pack of chewing gum, a pocketknife, and a handkerchief, and by the time you find him he's built a shelter and a canoe. From what I've read, his stories about Alaskan life and survival in the tundra would kink your hair. Well, not that yours needs curling."

This was Sophie's idea of a joke. Carrie's wild dark brown curls were the bane of her existence. She tamed them as best she could, but she often found herself the brunt of jokes over her out-of-control hair.

"Nash says he doesn't give interviews."

"Not just doesn't give interviews—this guy is like a ghost. No one has ever met or even talked to him."

"Surely his publisher or his editor—"

"No," Sophie said, cutting her off. "Everything has been done by computer."

"Well, then . . ."

"All anyone knows is that he lives near an Alaskan lake somewhere in the vicinity of the Arctic Circle."

"How is it you know so much about this guy?"

"I don't, and that's just it. No one does. The press has gone wild looking for him. Plenty of reporters have tried to track him down, without success. No one knows how to find him, and Finn Dalton doesn't want to be found. He should have called his book *Leave Me Alone*. Someone could pass him on the street and never know it was him, and from everything I've read, that's exactly how he likes it."

Intrigued, Carrie flipped through the pages of the book. "Nash said I could have any assignment I wanted if I got an interview from Finn Dalton."

"Of course he did. Nash has been around long enough to know he's got you in a no-win situation."

Carrie glanced up. "I don't care. I'm going to try."

"I hate to be a killjoy here, but Carrie, no way will you find this guy. Better reporters than either of us have tried and failed. Every newspaper, magazine, and media outlet is looking to dig up information about him, without success. Finn Dalton doesn't want to be found."

That might be the case, but Carrie refused to give up without even trying. This was far too important to drop just because it was a long shot. "I'm desperate, Sophie." And really, that said it all. If she was going to have a real career in journalism, she had to find Finn Dalton. Her entire future with the *Chicago Herald* hung in the balance.

"I admire your determination," Sophie murmured, "but I'm afraid you're going to hit one dead end after another."

"That might be the case." Carrie was willing to give her friend that finding Finn Dalton wouldn't be easy. "But I refuse to quit without trying." She knew Sophie didn't mean to be negative. "I want this chance, and if it means tracking Finn Dalton into some forsaken tundra, then I will put on my big-girl shoes and go for it." But not the heels she'd worn last night, that was for sure.

The first thing Carrie did in her search for Finn Dalton was read the book. Not once, but three times. She underlined everything that gave her a single hint as to his identity.

For two days she skipped lunch, spending her time on her computer, seeking any bit of information she could find that would help her locate Finn Dalton. She went from one search engine to another.

"How's it going?" Sophie asked as they passed each other on their way out the door a couple of days later.

"Good." Through her fact-finding mission, Carrie was getting a picture of the man who had written this amazing book. After a third read she almost felt as if she knew him. He hadn't always been a recluse. He'd been raised in Alaska and had learned to live off the land from his father, whom he apparently idolized. One thing was certain, he seemed to have no use for women. In the entire book, not once did he mention his mother or any female influence. It was more of what he didn't say that caught Carrie's attention.

"Any luck?" Sophie asked, breaking into her thoughts.

"Not yet." She hesitated. "Have you read the book?"

Sophie nodded. "Sure. Nearly everyone has."

"Did you notice he has nothing to say about the opposite sex? I have the feeling he must distrust all women."

Sophie shrugged, as if she hadn't paid much notice, but then she hadn't been reading between the lines the way Carrie had.

"How old do you think he is?" Sophie asked.

"I can't really say." Finn was an excellent writer and storyteller. But the stories he relayed could have happened at nearly any point in the last several decades. Current events were skipped over completely.

Sophie crossed her arms and looked thoughtful. "My guess is that he's fifty or so, to have survived on his own all these years."

Speculation wouldn't do Carrie any good. "Tell

you what. When I find out, you'll be the first to know. Deal?"

Sophie smiled and nodded. "Deal."

That night, as Carrie readied for her latest charity event, her cell rang. It was her mother in Seattle. They spoke at least two or three times a week. Carrie was tight with her family and missed them dreadfully.

"Hi, Mom," she answered, pressing her cell to her ear while she attempted to place a pearl earring into her earlobe.

"Hi, sweetheart. Are you busy?"

"I've got a couple of minutes." She switched ears and stabbed the second pearl into place before tucking her feet into a comfortable pair of high heels. She was scheduled to meet Harry in thirty minutes.

"Dad and I are so excited to see you at Thanksgiving."

"Yes, about that." Carrie grabbed her purse and tucked it under her arm while holding on to her phone. "Mom, I hate to tell you this, but there's a possibility I might not make it home for Thanksgiving."

"What?"

The disappointment in her mother's voice was painful to hear. "Have you ever heard of Finn Dalton?"

"Oh sure. Your father loved his book so much he

bought two additional copies. I read it, too. Now, that's a man."

"I want to interview him."

"Really. From what I understand, he doesn't give interviews."

"Yeah, that's what I heard, too."

"Does he ever come to Chicago?"

"Doubtful," Carrie murmured. If only it would be that easy and he would come to her. Well, that wasn't likely. Then again, something Sophie said had stayed in her mind. She could walk past him on the sidewalk and never know it was him. "I'll need to track Finn Dalton down, but I keep running into dead ends the same as everyone else." She mentioned her online search, the calls to Alaska, and the number of phones slammed in her ear. No one had been willing to talk to her. "I have to look at this from a different angle. Have you got any ideas?"

"From what your father said, Finn Dalton isn't a man who would enjoy being written up on the society page."

"That's just it, Mom. This would be an investigative piece. My editor told me I could have my pick of assignments if I was able to get this interview. It's important enough for me to take the vacation days I planned to use for Thanksgiving to find him."

"Oh Carrie, I hate the thought of you doing that."

"I know, I hate it, too, but it's necessary." Her mother was well aware of Carrie's feelings toward her current work situation.

"Do you really think you can find Finn Dalton?" her mother asked.

"I don't know if I can or not, but if I don't, it won't be from lack of trying."

"I've always admired your tenacious spirit. Can I tell your father you're going to write a piece on the man who wrote *Alone*?"

"Ah . . . not yet. I have to locate Dalton first."

"What have you discovered so far?" Her mother was nothing if not practical. Carrie could visualize her mother pushing up her shirtsleeves, ready to tackle this project with Carrie.

"Do you know where he was born?"

"No. I assumed it must have been Alaska, but there's no record of his birth there. I've started going through the birth records of other states, starting with the northwest, but haven't found his name yet." At this rate, it would be the turn of the next century before she found the right Dalton.

"What about his schooling? Graduation records?"

"I tried that, but he's not listed anywhere. Maybe he was home-schooled."

"You're probably right," her mother said, sounding proud that Carrie had reasoned it out. "One of his stories mentions his father mailing away for books, remember? Those were textbooks, I bet."

Carrie had made the same assumption.

"Finn is a rather unusual name, isn't it?" her mother continued softly, as though she was thinking out loud.

"And of course it could be a pseudonym, but his publisher claims the name is as real as the man." Nothing seemed the norm when it came to Finn Dalton.

"You know, work on the Alaskan pipeline was very big about the time your father and I got married. That was a huge project, and it brought a lot of men to Alaska; many of them stayed. His father might have been one of them."

"Yes." But that was a stab in the dark. She'd already spent hours going over every type of record she could think to research from Alaska, to no avail. Carrie glanced at the time, even though this talk was helping her generate ideas of where to continue looking for the mysterious Mr. Dalton.

"From what I remember, a lot of men left their wives and families for the attraction of big money."

"I could start looking at the employment records for the pipeline from that time period and see what I might find," Carrie said.

"That's a terrific idea. And listen, when you find Finn Dalton, make sure your dad gets a chance to chat with him, would you?"

"I can't promise that." First she'd need to convince Finn Dalton to talk to her!

"Just do your best."

"I'll do what I can."

"Bye, sweetie."

"Bye, Mom." Carrie ended the call and dumped her cell in her small bag. After a quick glance in the hallway mirror, she headed out the door to what she hoped would be one of the very last social events she would ever need to cover.

World Vision®

Building a better world for children

Knit for Kids

As a bestselling author and an avid knitter
with a big heart,
DEBBIE MACOMBER
proudly serves as the International Spokesperson
for World Vision's Knit for Kids.

Join Debbie and our nationwide family of
28,000 volunteer knitters to help fight poverty
with your knitting needles! You can give warmth
and comfort to children in need, across the
nation and around the world.

Visit **worldvision.org/knitforkids**
to download a pattern and start knitting today!

Visit **worldvision.org**
to see what else we're doing for children
around the world.